MW01592102

The Ghost

A NOVEL

by

K. Raymond Rush

DORRANCE
PUBLISHING CO
EST. 1920
PITTSBURGH, PENNSYLVANIA 15238

Dorrance Publishing Co
585 Alpha Drive
Pittsburgh, PA 15238
Visit our website at *www.dorrancebookstore.com*

ISBN: 978-1-6376-4173-6
eSIBN: 978-1-6376-4809-4

ACKNOWLEDGEMENTS

Mrs. Katherine Wiggs, Illustrator extraordinaire, for her patient and expert collaboration on the book cover and sketch for this novel. I found a great illustrator and a truly awesome friend. Contact her by email at: katherine.wiggs@gmail.com for a pleasant, professional experience in illustrating your work.

Friends and family that supported and encouraged me.
    The two women that God blessed me with. Elaine, deceased, that trusted my instincts and encouraged all my endeavors. Especially Barbe who pushed me to finish and follow through with this project. Her skills as a teacher are paramount in getting the material into a readable and hopefully enjoyable book.

Lastly, and most importantly, God, for putting the story into my heart. A story that lets everyone know we are all sinners, and if we will believe and call on Him, every person can have eternal life with Him and a much better here and now in this fleeting physical life.

1
Attacked

JJust five days short of his fourth birthday, the toddler lay in his father's arms with blood covering his little body. His father held him close and his mother sobbed and frantically reached for him. Turner Quincy Freeman (TQ), US Army Special Forces, retired early by a death fabricated by a government agency, a death more permanent than real, stood holding his son. Silent tears fell from his cheeks to mingle with the blood from his shoulder wound which flowed down to mix with the blood of his son. The wound was from an assassin's rifle.

A Purple Heart recipient and decorated for valor, TQ should have been wondering why he was attacked. He should have been perplexed at the identities of those behind the attack, but TQ knew, he knew all to well, who and why! He always feared it wasn't over, but hoped they would forget him, or he had lost them. He had left the *Team* sick of the killing and dead faces which floated through his dreams at night. The day he confronted the other six members of the Team, he knew this day might come, but he was alone at the time, almost five years ago.

He had felt it. It radiated from their eyes and bodies. Their fear of him transformed them into tight springs of uncertainty. They each knew the killing machine TQ had become by age twenty-three. That was years ago. Individually, they realized TQ could easily dispatch them, each a professional assassin respected in their own fields. His knowledge of their deeds, whereabouts, and alternate identities was prompting them to action. The fact he could and would kill more than half of them, if attacked openly, kept them at bay for that moment in time.

The first attack was a scant four hours later. Mike (Cypher) Ledbetter hated his name and only answered to 'Cypher.' Cypher monitored TQ's call for a taxi to go to Chicago's O'Hare airport for a flight to Phoenix, Arizona. The *Team* didn't know he planned to go back to the reservation, to another life that lay buried, and to claim a heritage of warriors long dead and a dignity of life that allowed a man to live in peace.

It isn't as hard as the common person thinks to get weapons of any sort on short notice, especially in Chicago's south side or among the abandoned warehouses of the lake shore. The *Team* was known only by their trademark MOs and their expertise at killing. They had to have a new method, one they had never used before.

Crimp (Porter Alexander Peterson) was born the third son of a Baptist minister in Mobile, Alabama. He was the *Team's* expert in electronics and explosives; trained in the basics as a Navy seal. Quiet and unobtrusive, slender but forceful by nature, he learned early blowing things up was more fun than the crossword puzzles he constantly finished. He was good at knitting – yes, knitting – which he did to keep his fingers and hands nimble for his real passion… creating unique explosives! Crimp made a hasty exit from the Navy and found his way into the Team three years earlier when a little present he made for Navy Commander Hartel only blew off the Commander's legs, but didn't kill him. It was the only other mistake he made until today. Ironically, it was the holiday tie he knitted two years ago for TQ that saved TQ's life. It would have been so exhilarating to kill the only man Crimp knew was better than he was with explosives. It angered him to think TQ escaped his bomb.

Getting a local junkie to shop for groceries and call a taxi to take the food to his apartment was easy. The junkie's apartment was only a half a block from where TQ was staying. The extra $500 the junkie could use for drugs was more than enough to convince him to leave that last small plastic sack in the trunk just behind the rear passenger door; the seat TQ always liked for quick entrance and exit from a vehicle.

The bomb trigger was a new twist on an old method. The bomb was made of plastic explosive molded into a semi-sphere crusted with wafers of 12-gauge steel. It had a simple battery through a mercury switch to a detonator which would go off when the semi-sphere bomb rolled over from a sudden stop or turn. The way taxi drivers in Chicago drive, it was a sure thing. The shaped charge would send the force and shrapnel, with parts of the car, all the way out the front windshield, taking pieces of TQ with it. It should have, except for that darn holiday tie!

It was five days before Thanksgiving and TQ planned to wear the tie this year like he had the past two years. The taxi arrived for TQ four minutes early, and TQ left the hotel literally on the run, with his bags in his right hand and the tie in the left. He quickly tossed the two carry-on bags onto the far side of the seat, followed by the holiday tie. He jumped in and gave directions to the driver to go to the airport, telling the driver to hurry and promising an extra twenty-dollar tip.

It was 3:30 P.M.. The cab driver thought the extra $20 this guy promised to give him for a quick ride would buy a Thanksgiving turkey for his wife and three kids. He decided to take a shortcut. Maybe he could get in one more fare before turning in his cab to the next shift. A left turn here and a quick right two blocks down would put him at the on-ramp toward the airport. The last thought the driver had as he made the quick right turn onto the ramp was, "Aahh, it was good to be alive."

TQ was reaching across the seat for the tie when the driver made the turn. The tie slid off the seat as TQ's weight threw him to the floor between the seats and the bomb went off. It made some cuts in his back muscles and started his clothes smoldering as some of the clothes in his bags settled back over him. The vehicle behind plowed into the wreckage which was flying back. This ignited a chain reaction that piled up fourteen vehicles in a hurry to get nowhere.

The first emergency vehicle to show up at the scene a scant ninety seconds later was a two-female traffic unit on the way back to the precinct for shift change. Sgt. Janet Hillsborough, approaching the car from the front, observed the wreckage and remains of the driver hanging on shards of windshield and across the hood. The left hand still gripped the steering wheel without the benefit of the arm for support.

Patrol person Anne Elizabeth Donner, three years on the force, had seen a lot, but nothing so violent as this. Pieces of the taxi were strewn about. Clothes from TQ's carry-on bags lay smoldering on top of what was part of the back seat and more lay in the street. She was just about to turn and check on the persons in the vehicles piled up behind the taxi when the smoldering clothes moved. Did she hear a moan? Anne literally jumped the eight feet to the taxi, loosening her service cap to expose strawberry blonde hair piled up in a professional manner.

TQ, like many other men, would have stopped to admire the 5'9" beauty who could have modeled had she not followed in the footsteps of a gruff old cop she loved, her father. He was still at the academy trying to cram 27 years of experience into the heads of rookie officers in just a few months so they could live past their first year on the streets of Chicago. He was her rock and the only man in her life. Her mother had died four days after Anne graduated from the academy. Not even two cops in the family could keep that thief, that cancer, from stealing her mother's life.

When Anne started throwing off the smoldering clothes from on top of TQ, she saw the raw burned skin and blood on his back. It touched her soul as only a woman of character and tenderness can be touched. For the moment the professional cop was gone. The head of thick dark brown, almost black, hair turned and she looked into the depths of eyes of velvet brown; eyes which seemed like wells with no bottom. She couldn't help herself. Confused by these sudden feelings, Anne bent and kissed each one of the eyes as the lids closed.

TQ had tried to move. He was wedged between what was left of the back and front seats. TQ wasn't sure what happened or where he was, but he thought he had seen an angel with strawberry blonde hair who kissed away the pain. Then, he just melted into the blackness your body accepts lest the pain overtake you.

At Anne's shout, Sgt. Hillsborough quickly assessed the plight of the large man wedged between the seats. "He may be broken badly and die if we move him. The traffic at this time of day will make emergency units very late in arriving, maybe too late. There is an emergency clinic at the Academy only three miles away, just past the airport."

Deciding the risk was necessary; Sgt Hillsborough grabs two burly, muscular men in construction gear standing in the growing crowd and directs them in the extraction of TQ from the wreckage.

2
Rescued

Anne wheeled the squad car through the debris so the men could load TQ into the back seat of the car. The two officers sped off with the bloody man across the back seat as more squad cars and the first ambulance arrived at the scene.

A man on a motorcycle watched intently through the darkened visor in his helmet. Peeper had a photographic memory and no concept of right or wrong. If it was good for Peeper, John Carter the Third, then it must be right. Death was mandatory so not to worry about when it is time to kill someone. What now shocked the mind of Peeper was he saw TQ move. TQ had somehow survived what no one could or should. It made the hair on his neck stand up so he scrunched his shoulders and moved his head from side to side to relieve himself of the premonition, the chill of death and doom. He had to follow the patrol car to see where they took him. The Team had to be told as soon as possible of their failure to kill their leader. They would be furious, for sure! For himself, he felt a growing sense of doom blossoming in the pit of his stomach.

"That's crazy!" He admonished himself. Sure, TQ was a phenomenon, extraordinary even, but he was human. TQ was the one who trained them into a unit of one mind and force. That training would be TQ's downfall, Peeper was sure. He forced a smile, but the feeling of disaster which gripped him didn't go away. It felt like something sharp was grinding away at his insides.

The ride to the academy seemed to take hours as Anne's rearview mirror revealed the shallow breathing of the large man folded across the back seat. "He can't die like this!" Anne whispered. Then, she caught her partner, Janet, looking at her intently and realized she had spoken out loud. *So what*, she thought to herself. *And why was the squad car so hot anyway?*

The cold air rushing in through the door hit Anne hard as she jumped from the car to assist the two people in white uniforms waiting with a gurney. She felt the heat on her neck and face again as she slid her arms under his chest to lift him and help get the mystery man onto the gurney. She felt unfamiliar desperation and confusion as they rushed him into the clinic. Anne followed as far as the nurse would let her.

Dr. Alfred Bailey had seen his share of wounds and tragedy in Vietnam and during thirty plus years patching up police officers for the greater Chicago area. He often talked of getting into private practice in a quiet little town somewhere, but the truth was he liked knowing in these moments of trauma it was only him and God who kept death away from people like this.

"Like this," he mused out loud to no one. As he worked on TQ, he acknowledged to himself in all his years of practice, he had only seen about a half dozen men with a body finely tuned like an animal, like that of a tiger. His instinct made him acknowledge the tiger lying unconscious beneath his hands now would wreak revenge on those who had tried to trap and kill him. He also knew they, whoever *they* were, would try again, soon. He had to get this man back to where he could defend himself because warriors like this fought alone and, if needed, died alone. Their one weakness, the hero trait, was they would never abandon their friends or family. They would stay, even if it meant sure death, while taking a heavy toll on the enemy. Yes, if he died, his enemy would remember him, probably even respect and admire him.

Dr. Bailey directed, "Nurse, let's cover these burns and get something to help him rest. The man in the bed was like a magnificent tiger. Animals like this recover best from injury while sleeping."

Janet had grabbed Anne's arm to stop her from pacing the hallway and explained they had to go back to the precinct and clock out. They were an hour over now and the operations sergeant was having a fit about not having completed reports in his hands.

As she turned to follow her partner, Anne was startled to see her father, Lt. Fred Donner, lounging in the doorway observing her closely. He gave her his half smile, a small wave, and went back down the hall. She thought she knew her dad well, but couldn't read the face he was wearing now.

In the meantime, Peeper had made his way along the coast of Lake Michigan to the new safe house west of Chicago. No one except Spooky Harris had thought it was necessary. He had insisted. He had one of the *feelings* he experienced about plans they made. His *feelings* had often warned them, saved their collective and individual hides, as it were. Everyone respected Spooky Harris' *feelings*. They didn't know how or why it worked and didn't care. Harris wasn't just superstitious, he was gifted this way.

He was also an expert with any long gun. It was like he was part of the weapon, as if his brain was directing the bullet to its mark. He always shot to the head from the side. He didn't want dead eyes looking at him in his dreams every night. Harris was just opening a fresh Lablatt Blue beer when Peeper came silently through the door. Spooky's loud "Awe crap!" brought the rest of the Team to immediately confront Peeper. As Peeper hesitated to speak, Harris let out with another "Awe crap!" and turned away to lean down, head in his hands on the kitchen counter.

The faces of the *Team* members showed expressions from disbelief, anger, puzzlement, and worry as Peeper gave them the details.

Latoya (Toy) White, an ebony beauty with a heart of ice, calculated the cost and losses as only a professional CPA can. She suggested another attack while the enemy they had just created was wounded and vulnerable.

Toy asked, "Peeper, where did the cops take TQ?"

Peeper blurted out, "I followed that squad car to the Chicago Police Academy. He looked in bad shape when they snatched him from what was left of that taxi."

"So, how do we get to him? It has to be soon. If we wait, he'll disappear and come after us in his own time. That Indian has more patience than *Job*. He will wait as long as it takes to get back at us," stated Toy.

Ricco, the Team hothead, interjected, "Hey Toy, can you get Crimp and me some uniforms like those the rookies wear? The cops might alert to new beat cops arriving, but not to a couple of new rookies walking around like they were lost. With a little accelerant we have, Crimp could rig something small, but powerful enough to give TQ a right efficient cremation at no cost to the government, except the building he's in."

Cypher said, "I'll have the floor plans and security deciphered in about an hour."

Spooky straightened and said, "I don't like it, but I'm with you. We must finish this now!"

Ricco glanced in Spooky's direction and caught the look of near panic as Spooky turned to the table and poured a half glass of bourbon instead of Lablatt Blue. It was the very same bourbon TQ sipped when he was leading this team instead of being its target.

3
The Ghost Is Gone

Dr. Bailey finished checking his patient. As he prepared to leave for the evening, he thought, *This guy, whoever he is, is almost healing under my eyes. What kind of man gets attacked like that? He isn't a political figure or a known crime figure. The prints Lt. Donner ran came back no match. It's like he doesn't exist. That can't be. He is probably foreign and we don't have access to the files.* Another long look at his patient sleeping peacefully on his stomach somehow assured Dr. Bailey this man was not the enemy. It also made him very glad he was not an enemy of the sleeping tiger.

It was several hours after his check out time and past his supper when Lt. Fred Donner hit the send key on the email to his old military and fishing buddy, Col. Paul Stanton, U.S. Army Criminal Investigation Division Headquarters (CID) in Washington, D.C. He knew Paul had assets and contacts to find out just who this guy was and what they were up against. Why did he care who this guy was? The answer was easy – she was walking into his office that very second. He had recognized the look Anne had bestowed on the unconscious man. It was the same look her mother had reserved for him. A man never forgets the birth of love and commitment pouring from a woman's soul like a soft warm light which comforts a man's heart and challenges him to be her everything.

When picked up, it's a challenge which can never be put down. He knew he couldn't stop it, but he could put a stop to the unknown man if he meant harm to Anne. Well, maybe he could. There was something both honest and ominous about the man lying on the bed just down the hall. He had reached the same conclusions Doc had about the man. Be cool and be careful – very careful!

Fred smiled, "Hi Honey, what brings you back here?"

Washington, D.C.

Col. Paul Stanton was just about to the door when the watch person hollered the bell on his computer was going off. That bell was set to go off for emails from about only a dozen important sources. With a sigh and squaring of his shoulders, he realized it was things like this that cost him his marriage. No woman should be left alone night after night. Only a unique woman could understand the call of duty he had to his country. Where was she? Did she exist? Probably not!

Whoa! Donner's message was concise, but laden with information, questions, and a tone full of fatherly concern. This involved Anne, Paul's god-daughter. Anne was like the child he never had. Whoever this guy was had better come up clean or he would wish he had never been born! Time to call in some favors! Heck, for this he would probably owe some favors, maybe a lot of favors.

The Police Academy

Two clean-cut rookie cops, AWOL bags in hand, joked with the guard and intently listened to his description of the activities and directions to different facilities. The guard was very helpful. It was the only time the guard felt his job was meaningful, when he helped the rookies as they arrived. Look how they hung on his every word. By the end of three months it would just be a slight wave of acknowledgement.

He answered their last question with, "What's that? Yeah, we have a clinic. It's building C-120. Go around the corner. It's the third building on the right with the big parking lot in front. There's probably nobody there except a nurse or orderly at this time of night." The two rookies thanked him for the information and strolled in that direction.

They'll make good cops someday, the guard thought to himself.

Peeper drove the van from his position half a block away from the guard shack and made his way around to park on the street directly across from the back side of building C-120 for a quick getaway. There was no one else around. The street was empty. Nothing was left to chance this time. The device would be planted where it would successfully eliminate TQ and set off remotely after Crimp and Ricco reached the van. He was going to have to tell Spooky those new cameras and audio miniatures really worked well. This operation was looking easy. It would be good to be able to sleep tonight without worrying about TQ sneaking up on them like a ghost in the middle of the night. He always moved like a ghost, so quiet you would wonder if he had really been near you at all. Sometimes it gave Crimp the creeps as he watched TQ move and listened intently to hear him make a sound, any sound.

As Anne and her father entered the room where TQ was, her heart was beating like she just finished a five-mile run. Why? She didn't even know the name of this mystery man. Anne reached to quietly pull back the curtain so as not to disturb the mystery man. Her father snatched the curtain all the way back with a series of oaths, totally out of character for him; words which would make a sailor blush. Anne was shocked almost as much by her father's reaction as she was by the empty bed. The bloody bandage under the window confused both Anne and her Father for a moment. The mystery man was so hurt. How could he disappear? Where had he gone? Anne stood looking at the empty bed with the neatly folded covers as her father stormed out the door to alert everyone of the man's disappearance.

Fred Donner could not imagine how a man tore up like that could get up and leave. The folded covers at the foot of the bed; the man left no detail unattended, even in his bad condition.

The two new rookies he almost ran over in the hall stood with shocked expressions as he briefly explained about the man and his disappearance. They eagerly left in the directions he pointed out as the most likely routes of escape. Lt. Donner continued down the hall to spread the alarm. He thought, *They'll make good cops when they graduate. I must remember to get their names.*

TQ had awakened to pain up and down his back. He had to figure out what had happened to him, how he got here, how badly he was hurt, and how to get out of here. TQ had to do something with his hands as he thought about his situation, so he folded the hospital blankets and made the bed despite the pain like constant fire on his back. He was having some trouble hearing. He was also having a slight problem with his equilibrium. Explosions do that sort of thing to a person. To say he was lucky or had a miracle was an understatement. He had been thinking lately about the reality of God. It was one of the main reasons he wanted to get out. He was unsure of a lot of things in his life. He had to get answers. He had to get out of here and go to ground, hide where no one could find him. TQ had places and money cached no one else knew of. Now he was glad he had made special arrangements over the past few years. This was his old *Team's* work, and good work it was. If it hadn't been for that silly tie, he'd be dead for hours already. Had he really thought they would, or even could, allow him to just quit and move into a quieter life, a normal life? Maybe he should have told the *Team* his reasons. No, the reasons were private, his reasons.

It was a wish, a desire, to be done with killing for hire. The government he worked for could not acknowledge him, or the *Team* members, if they got caught on a mission. They certainly wouldn't help him now. Would they get involved in any way? No, not unless it might cause a security breach. Then, they would send out enough others to take out the whole Team in short order. You can't go against the whole system. It was just too large and too efficient. The same people who gave them Intel and paid them millions of dollars had them on their wanted list. They kept them way down on the bottom, just for show, but they were still there.

Voices coming down the hall! RRRIIIP! One bandage was torn off of his back and thrown at the base of the window to add confusion and make them think he exited by that method. TQ slipped quickly into the closet and left the door slightly ajar so he could watch the room. TQ didn't like to be surprised. The pain was mentally pushed aside as this potentially deadly situation developed. His heritage and training made it almost automatic.

THAT FACE!! The angel in his dream wasn't a dream. For once, TQ couldn't move. He did not know what to do even after the big Lieutenant ran out of the room ranting and raving. He just stood behind the door with one eye drinking in the beauty of the strawberry blonde hair cascading down over a dark green sweater. That she was beautiful was a no-brainer! That he had never met her was easy to accept. What perplexed him and held him at bay was wondering why this angel of a woman had kissed him during his most vulnerable moment in life. It must have been her who took care of him. Why?

Wait a minute! That big guy was a cop. Was he under guard? Where was this place? Despite the pain of his back, TQ remained immobile. Only his eye at the crack in the door moved over every inch of the stunning woman before him. He memorized every detail from the beautiful sparkling eyes, sensitive lips, and the figure which started a pulse pounding that had nothing to do with his back. Shocked, he watched her eyes fill with tears that slid glistening down her cheeks. Were they for him? If only they were, but he didn't even know this woman. Get a grip! The big guy's back and is he mad. He snatched the decoy bandage off the floor. What did he just say? He called her Anne. The angel's name is Anne!

Washington, D.C.

It was exactly 2012 hours, 8:12 P.M., as the first of a flood of information which supposedly DIDN'T exist came pouring over the secure means to Col. Paul Stanton. The Intel he had in his hands wiped away the exhaustion of a 20 hour day like a summer shower clears the air. He knew the *Teams* he was reading about existed, but only as rumors. Col. Stevens did not like what they did. He did recognize the necessity of what they did for the safety of his country. You fight unorthodox enemies in unorthodox ways. Sometimes killing is the only way. This *Team* is especially efficient, used only on the toughest jobs. The more it unraveled the more he wished he was not involved. If he wasn't very, very careful he would end up very dead! How did Fred Donner get into this mess, anyway? Oh yeah, Anne, a woman grown now! Women can get men into all kinds of trouble, even fathers and god-fathers. Col. Stanton fired up the cross cut shredder and eliminated all the documents as fast as he could memorize the important information.

Six hours twenty-eight minutes and 201 pages later, he breathed a sigh of relief and wondered what he could tell Fred. How could he get this information to him? Personally, that was the only safe way. He would fly into Chicago and pick up some artillery right off the plane. Call in another marker with a friend in the FBI. Call Fred from the airport or surprise him? I'll play that by ear! No, better by phone, or maybe not. Use the code set up long ago, *'The fish are biting. Let's hit the lake.'* Donner would know he was coming and be prepared for good or bad news. He would be at Donner's house before Fred got home from work.

Back in Chicago

Ricco and Peeper kept talking to Spooky as they searched the compound, with 76 other recruits and cadre from the Academy, for the missing mystery man. TQ had vanished. Ricco was amazed! Peeper was incredulous and Spooky kept repeating foul expletives to relieve his frustration. When the search was called off after two hours, Ricco and Spooky slipped away with Peeper. They had to inform the others of TQ's new vanishing act. The Ghost was gone again.

Almost two hours into the search, Fred Donner walked back into the clinic room to find Anne sitting on the bed clutching the pillow to her breast, head bowed, and her strawberry blond hair down around her face. She could not understand her own confusion and feelings of loss. With a biting tone in his voice, Fred said, "Anne, get a grip and think. I want you to get into that Jetta and go home." In a softened tone, her Dad added, "Get some sleep. You have duty at 0600. I'm not sure when I'll get home. We are ordering pizza for a task force being set up from the local precinct. The state police are sending investigators. We must figure out what is happening and to whom. How can a guy that big, that hurt, just vanish? No one even saw him. It has us all baffled! He disappeared like some spirit or ghost or something."

Anne, slipping off the bed and sighing deeply, replied, "OK, Dad." She turned back toward the bed, placed the pillow in its proper place and smoothed it gently with her hands. Anne turned toward the door, still looking down, a deep frown on her face.

Fred said, "I'd walk you to your car, but I have to check on the weapons room again. I have a feeling our mystery man is dangerous enough without weapons. I don't want him to get his hands on anything that will give him another advantage. It seems that he is already invisible."

Anne quietly replied, "I have to stop in the Ladies room, then I'll go straight home. I promise!"

Donner gave his daughter a hug, a peck on the forehead, and a long look at arms length before he left the room just ahead of his daughter.

TQ slipped silently into the hall after Anne and ducked into the office marked *Dr. Bailey*. Just as he figured, the good doctor had several changes of clothes in a closet for emergencies in Chicago's changing weather. The pants were a little short, the shirt wouldn't button across his broad chest and, believe it or not, the shoes were a little too big.

The goose down jacket he put on over the shirt was snug but warm. The old Chicago Cubs ball cap would cover his head and alter his identity. TQ was walking past the Ladies room when he heard the toilet flush. He hurriedly zipped the jacket. The sound of the flushing toilet meant Anne didn't beat him to the parking lot. He had to find her car before Anne exited the building. How many Jetta cars were in the parking lot? He couldn't afford to be standing in the parking lot for more than 30 seconds or he would be discovered.

Finding Anne's car was easy. It was the only Jetta there, parked almost in front of the door. What if it was locked as it should be? He had no tools and no time. The passenger side was unlocked. TQ thought, *Whoever is looking out for me, 'Thanks'*. He slid over the front seat into the back seat just as Anne came out of the door into the parking lot.

Had she imagined a shadowy movement in her car! Maybe it was just the play of the parking lot lights. Anne made it look as if she was trying to find her keys in the bottom of her purse as she retrieved the small automatic pistol she carried as a back-up. Not large in size, the Glock .40 caliber would stop anyone dead at that range. She couldn't miss inside the car. If there was someone there, they were trapped. The driver side door opened easily under her hand....

Meanwhile, Lt. Donner was worried because no one knew of the two new recruits he described or what became of them. It was obvious, now, they came looking for the mystery man. It was very doubtful they were looking to rescue him. That left only one option – elimination! Come to think of it, they were carrying bags, but it was after in-processing hours. A chill went up Donner's back to think some wise guys dared to come right into the sanctum of the Chicago Police Academy. The first issue would be tightening security. It will start with reeducating the gate guards!

Spooky, Ricco, and Peeper were bombarded with questions as they arrived at the safe house on the lake. Only the chill of a late November wind cut short the questions in the doorway. The conversation moved to the kitchen where left-over Chinese take-out and beer provided a late supper for the unsuccessful team members. TQ had vanished! He eluded them as easily as if he were actually a Ghost, earning again, the nickname they gave him.

At the end of an hour and a half of rehashing the whole scene for the flaws in their failed plan, Cypher expressed their collective feelings, "What the hell are we going to do now?"

Peeper pulled one of his favorite knives, from who knows where, and checked the edge. Somehow, he felt it was going to get really close and personal in the near future.

Washington, D.C.

It's now 0430 hours (4:30 A.M.) and Col. Stanton was packing the essentials for the trip, one suit case, and a tube with fishing rods. He and Fred were old fishing buddies. The best place to exchange information and plan this war was in a boat on Lake Michigan. Why did he think it would be a war? There was no declared enemy and no weapons seen except that one bomb which took out a taxi driver that had a wife and three kids under ten years old. The driver had quickly been cleared as the target. It had to be the mystery man. Got to get to the airport to catch the first flight! Sleeping on the flight was almost his normal method for rest and relaxation.

Back in Chicago

As Anne opened the door to the Jetta, she slid on to the seat with her back to the steering wheel while her Glock and face poked over the back of the seat. The first thing she saw was TQ's deep, velvet brown eyes. She breathed a soft 'Ohhhh' as TQ gently removed the gun from her hand.

They simply stared into each other's eyes for the longest 15 seconds in history. During this time of charged emotions, as they stared into each other's eyes, not a word was spoken. Suddenly, TQ realized anyone viewing the scene would correctly assume he was hiding in the car. They would also assume Anne was in danger, though he knew he could never hurt her in any way. That scenario would write a tragedy Shakespeare never dreamed of. He released the soft hand he had been holding and placed the Glock back into it.

TQ explained, "If we are seen, take me into custody. I'll be gone in less than an hour."

Anne did not doubt his statement one bit. Their hearts had just exchanged a special love through their eyes. They didn't even know the other person's name! Still, it was true, it was real. It only happens once in a lifetime, to a very few people. Could she trust him? Would she trust him? Absolutely! In her heart, Anne realized this was the man she had been waiting for, the man God had given her for the rest of her life.

Anne had an overwhelming desire to talk to her mother. If only she hadn't died so young! Anne knew her mom would have understood. Anne had her father's strength and her mother's perception. How could this wonderful, confusing, exciting, scary thing be happening? She turned in the seat, buckled up, and left the parking lot for home. She never said a word! As she drove, her mind dwelled on her mother, to that time when she doubted God, His promises, His care, His enduring love. Mom had helped rebuild her faith through a long night of tears, seeking, and, finally, joy.

Anne got her physical beauty from her mother. Both were stunning, but clueless as to why they received so much attention. Her spiritual beauty came from the teaching of both parents, and a full acceptance of every facet of God's presence, power, and love from her childlike faith.

Anne's mother wasn't supposed to be the one to get sick. Mother's don't get sick. When she started to feel 'woozy' in the head with headaches, it was attributed to blood pressure problems, or maybe a bump on the head. Then, about a month later, the problems using her left leg and arm started. She couldn't lift her leg to get into the car. Sometimes she stumbled for no reason. About the same time, she lost control of her left arm and hand. She would knock things over when she reached out with her left hand. There was a lot of spilled water and coffee at the dinner table.

The family doctor sent her for MRIs, from head to toe. The results showed Glioblastoma. This malignant brain cancer is incurable. A year, two on the outside, was what four different doctors said. The news was devastating to Anne and her father. Her mother was the strong one. Relying totally on God, she found peace as she trusted, whatever the outcome, it would be the best God had for her.

Anne's mother told her in confidence to be strong and take care of Fred, Anne's father. They had been together for over thirty years, in "harness" as they worked together to honor God in their house and as they walked through the world.

Anne watched as her father, a big tough cop, would sit by the hospital bed and read to her mother, or just hold her hand as she slept. The pain became worse day to day, week to week, month after month. Then the pain stopped at 2:05 A.M. four days after Anne graduated from the police academy. Anne tried to be the strong daughter her mother wanted her to be. She was successful during the day, but each night she lay in bed and talked and cried out to God, asking why. God never answered why, but his peace would suddenly come and Anne would rest the night through; rest in the arms of God just as her mother was doing.

What had just happened? TQ wasn't entirely sure, but he knew it was at least part of what he was looking for when he quit the *Team*. Anne was part of the answer to all those months of restlessness and wondering why he was, what he was to do with his life. TQ knew Anne was in his future, if he had one. He watched from between the front seats as Ann turned left out of the parking lot and made her way across town to a white cape cod with maroon shutters and a detached two-car garage. It would have been easier to get into the house if the garage were attached to the house. A question crept into TQ's mind, *What's missing in my life?*

TQ was about to get out of the car when Anne whispered, "Stay down! Uncle Dale lives next door and watches our place like a hawk when I'm here alone. Dad and I fish a lot from our cabin on Lake Michigan. I'll be awhile getting food, medicine, and some fishing poles. Then we'll get you settled in at the lake cabin until we figure out what to do about your problem, whatever that is."

TQ explained the clothes he was wearing didn't fit. Anne said she would get some of her father's old clothes when they arrived at the cabin on the lake. Most would fit, if imperfectly. TQ was wider across the chest than her father, and a little taller.

In the seventeen minutes Anne was gone, TQ spotted Uncle Dale glancing out the window of his house not twenty feet away. TQ thought, *Nice of him to care. Family, that's what it's all about.* All he had left was a great-aunt, Two Flowers, but they weren't close. They hadn't talked in over three years. He couldn't afford to have family in his profession, for their sakes.

"I want out. I want a normal life with a wife and kids, lots of kids."

This was whispered to the back of a front seat in the Jetta. True to his heritage, TQ stoically ignored the pain in his back, the sting and burning that ran down the full length of his back. He only wondered if it would slow him down when it came time to act. He knew the time was coming. He had to be ready when this blew up in his face!

Col. Stanton arrived at O'Hare Airport at 0855, picked up his bag and pole tube, and headed for the rental car line. A soft ladylike voice spoke his name directly behind him. His contact was 5'3" and had brown hair with auburn highlights wound into a tight bun at the back of her head. The tan, loose fitting business suit did nothing to impress the man. To himself he said, "Typical career woman with no private life." As she turned and led the way toward a dark blue Chevy Blazer parked just outside the door, he couldn't help wonder what she would look like dressed for dinner. She was attractive, for sure. It looked to Col. Stanton as if the woman took pain to hide the good looks God gave her.

"Your package is behind the driver's seat." She tossed him the keys and turned toward a bright yellow Ford pick-up truck.

"What's your name?" he asked.

She threw over her shoulder, "Isn't pertinent," as she climbed into the truck. She turned her head and saw he was still watching her. "Katherine. Not Kathy or Kate…Katherine!" She calmly started the vehicle and drove away while he stood still and watched with a perplexed look on his face.

Katherine! Katie suits her better. I like it, he thought. Then he asked no one and everyone out loud, "Katherine who?"

Forty-five minutes later, Col. Stanton pulled into his old friend's driveway and waved to Uncle Dale as he exited the rented, blue Blazer. He had his own door key. Uncle Dale waved back and left the window, satisfied he had done his duty.

For the next several hours, he busied himself getting gear properly stowed in Fred's big fishing boat. He made sure he included such staples as sardines, chips, beer, lunchmeat, and bread. He was on his third trip to the boat when Donner hollered out, "What are you two doing in the boat already?" Immediately every sense in Col. Stanton's body became alert. He returned with, "Fred, Anne's not here. Isn't she working?"

Donner stopped dead in his tracks. His face was as white as the boat he was standing next to. "No! I called her precinct, but they said she had called in and asked for time off due to the recent traumatic things she had witnessed. When I pulled up, I naturally thought she was here with you."

Like stereo, the two men loudly expressed the same question at the same moment, "Where is she?"

4
Planning!

Ken (Spooky) Harris took a deep breath and said, "Ok, let's get a round table working. We need to have someone in charge that we all agree on. We must run this like any other operation. We were sloppy twice. If we aren't ready the next time, TQ surely will be ready. In fact, we have to consider that TQ is already hunting us. That's not a pleasant thought, now is it? That means we have to implement defensive plans as well as offensive or we will seal our own fates." It was the most anyone had heard him say since this all started. There was no denying the wisdom of his words or the hint of uneasiness in his voice.

After a brief discussion, Peeper was sent out in the cold November wind to find another safe house while the rest of the team tore down and prepared to move out at a moment's notice. *Not much sleep tonight for sure*, Pepper thought as he yawned loudly. Nerves were frayed and tempers were close to flaring. In the Bible it says, "The wicked will flee when there is no one chasing them." Fear had a hold of the normally cool team. They were running! They were sure 'The Ghost' was just around the next corner!

The late November moon shone bright through the windows of the Jetta. Flattering flashes of light danced across the face and hair of the angel driving the small car through the cold windy night. Why did TQ still think of her that way? She had become TQ's personal angel. The car's heater gently blew the scent of her hair and perfume to him. They were things he had never noticed about any other woman. He was suddenly aware he had relaxed. TQ was actually content just riding in a cramped car with the pain of a burned back and taking in the scent of this beautiful woman he knew only as Anne. He didn't care if they ever arrived at their destination. They could drive all night!

About 45 minutes west of the city, Anne turned right on a secondary road for a couple of miles, then a left and the next right onto a road along Lake Michigan. The road was lined with cottages on one side and docks and boat houses on the lake side. Anne pulled into the driveway of a well-kept older cottage with an attached garage. A few stray snowflakes landed on Anne's face as she exited the car.

Anne wanted the mystery man to wait until she had carried all the food and gear into the house before getting out of the car. She quickly learned this man was used to being in charge and had his own ideas. Strangely, she liked him being in charge. It was comforting, but strange. The only indication of the pain TQ was in was a stiffening of his back as he picked up bags of food and two suitcases of clothes at the same time. He never flinched or made a sound as he made his way to the cottage door just behind Anne.

Every minute Anne spent with the big, silent, mystery man convinced her he was the reason she had been waiting. He was the one. "God, let it be him," she breathed quietly.

Her parents had instilled in her she was one special woman created for one special man. She had gotten discouraged in the last six months, almost given up on the special man God had for her. Instead, Anne had told God it was in his hands. She knew in her heart it was happening now. The waiting was over, or was it? Anne was stopped short by shocking thoughts, *What if he had to leave? What if he were killed?* Most women would have collapsed at the thought. Anne just got mad! She said to herself, "No way! I found him and I'm keeping him!" She never considered he might be a bad person, that maybe he wasn't the man God had for her.

They entered the kitchen of the cabin quickly.

"Do you want to eat before I look at your back, or should we change the bandage first?" Anne asked as she reached to turn up the thermostat. Food! When was the last time he had fueled his big frame? TQ simply said, "Eat first." To himself he mused, "Efficient, but not bossy; very nice!" After all these years by himself, you would think he could cook. He didn't even make good scrambled eggs. His quick search of the small but comfortable kitchen revealed the dishes, flatware, pots, and pans. Setting the table he could do as Anne set out the food she had brought from her home. Leftover meat loaf, salt potatoes, and string beans never tasted so good. This lovely lady could cook! He was half way through his third helping when he realized Anne was sitting across from him, chin in her left hand, just smiling at him. TQ asked around a mouthful of food, "What, you never saw a grown man eat before?"

Anne's smile turned into a chuckle, then into a lilting laugh which sent TQ's heart racing. The more one laughed, the more the other laughed until TQ was holding his hands to his back to try and relieve the pain caused by the movement to the laughter. A few giggles between pauses and Anne got control of herself before TQ did.

5
Introductions!

When Anne could catch her breath, she said, "We better get those bandages changed. It's getting late and you need to rest. I know the Bible says laughter is the best medicine, but it looked like you were dying from the pain of laughing just a moment ago. You better watch what you do!"

Anne emphasized this with a grin and a wiggling finger in his face. When she turned and went into the bathroom, TQ just got up and followed. It seemed natural. It seemed very right.

Anne put the lid down on the toilet and pointed to it. She directed, "Sit facing the wall and take that shirt off. You can sponge bath later. Here, let me help," she expressed as she reached toward his shirt.

TQ just tightened his jaw as his shirt and bandages were removed and the waves of pain ran up and down his back.

Anne's experienced eye surveyed the new wounds and took in all of the old ones. There was evidence of a bullet going through the muscle of the upper right arm and three clean straight scars like knife wounds on the left ribs. *Someday*, she thought, *this man will tell me all about these scars, old and new*. For now she would hold her peace. She worked quickly to limit his pain. TQ sat rigid, bent over the top of the tank. Outwardly, he showed no emotion that would reflect the pain he felt.

Anne asked, "Since I'm your get-away driver, cook, nurse, and housekeeper, we should at least be able to call each other by our given names. What's yours?"

TQ answered with, "Your name is Anne. I'm called TQ. My real name is Turner Quincy Freeman. I'm a full-blooded Navajo boy that's a long way from the reservation. I just wanted to go back to the reservation, to a simpler life."

Anne queried, "What happened? Why are people, someone, trying to kill you? I'm sorry, it's not my business. If it's bad, the law could make me testify about it and... and I'm a cop. And, how do you know my name?"

TQ responded quietly, "I know." TQ smiled in a way which sent warmth all the way down to Anne's toes. "It doesn't matter, as you never read me my rights. It would be inadmissible evidence. While everyone was looking all over that campus, I was in the closet watching you. I heard the big cop, your father I guess, call you by your name."

Anne just smiled back and, shaking her head slightly, crossed the hall to her dad's bedroom and opened the closet door. She extracted a faded blue flannel shirt her dad hardly ever wore because it was too big for him.

Anne suggested, "Here, try this on." She held it up against his chest to see of it would fit. Her pulse started racing again and she could feel the red creep up her neck and across her face. What she didn't realize was the effect of her touch on TQ. "It's late. I'll get you a towel and washcloth for that sponge bath. While you do that, I'll do dishes. I'll get cleaned up for bed after I get the sick boy tucked into bed."

TQ didn't even mind the tone of motherly control. He rather enjoyed it. It was nice being looked after like that. How long had it been? Maybe never! He couldn't remember his mother. She had died while he was just a toddler. An ache was there that never could not be filled.

TQ felt safe for the time being. How long this feeling would last he couldn't even guess. It would be best to leave as soon as he could, unless something unexpected happened. He had to protect Anne from the trouble he brought with him. If he felt up to it, he would leave after breakfast in the morning. How? He had no money close at hand, no ID, no transportation, nothing within quick access! It would take more time to get to one of his special caches. Did he have the time? Anne knocked once on the bathroom door. She opened it enough to slide just her hand in to give him a new toothbrush.

TQ thought, *This woman thinks of everything*!

TQ took his time, enjoying the feelings of peace and love. *Love*, where did that word come from? "It came from my heart, yeah, love." This realization caused TQ to stare at the large steely-eyed man in the mirror. For the first time, he felt he did not know who he was or what he was supposed to be doing with his life. It seemed as if he was no longer in control. If not him, then who was in control!

TQ entered the kitchen buttoning his new shirt just as Anne was finishing the dishes. The shirt was snug, but he got it buttoned finally. Everything was put away in its respectful place, tidy and neat. He remembered the great tasting food and asked, "Is there any more of that meat loaf left?"

Anne couldn't help grinning as she gently scolded, "You already brushed your teeth!"

TQ grinned back and held up his fingers like a good Boy Scout and said, "Promise, I'll do them again before bed."

Anne replied with mock sternness and a raised brow, "The cook is done. Clean up after yourself." Then she placed more meatloaf, bread, and potatoes before this seemingly bottomless pit.

Before she left him alone with the meatloaf to get ready for bed, Anne paused to say, "I called in to the station. I told them I was traumatized by all the events and was taking a week of my vacation. After all, I'm a poor emotional woman. I wanted to wait to ask you but it was getting late. Was my decision to call in ok?"

TQ nodded, "Yeah, thanks for telling me. I don't know why, but I trust you. I think I'll have some coffee instead of juice."

With an exaggerated sigh and shaking of the head, Anne said, "No, you have juice. You need all the sleep you can get... no caffeine!"

As TQ grinned and looked to where the coffee pot sat, Anne bolted across the kitchen to block his access to it. Just as Anne reached the counter, she was swept high in the air by TQ's arms. The shriek of delight Anne heard was her own. TQ spun her around in mid air as if she were a child. He pulled her to his chest with arms like steel and a gentle touch like a feather brushing her skin. Her breath caught as he gently kissed her eyes, hair, nose, and finally her mouth. Anne met him there, giving all that she was getting. Long minutes later, they stood looking into each other's eyes, smiling silly smiles only people in love can make.

Lord, is this too soon, too fast? Show me and guide me, Anne silently prayed. TQ cocked his head and slowly said: "I'll get us... juice."

They sat on the couch watching old movies on the television. Anne sat with her legs up to the side, leaning into TQ's chest until the gentle deep rhythm told her he had fallen asleep from exhaustion brought on by the day's events. She gently extricated herself from his arms. Anne rose and put a pillow under his head, then covered him with a quilt her grandmother had made. Quietly, she put herself to bed. It was late and she was exhausted. Still, sleep didn't come for another 20 minutes. Anne's mind kept looking into soft velvet brown eyes.

6
War Declared!

Paul looked at his old friend and urgently said, "Call Uncle Dale! Do it now!"

Uncle Dale reported he had initially thought someone else was in the back seat of the car, but had changed his mind after checking several times. Anne had been in and out of the house, bringing supplies and fishing gear like she had done the last twenty some years. He supposed she was going to the cottage on the lake.

Without a word, the two friends hitched up the boat and finished loading supplies for a week. The added supplies now included body armor, hand guns and ammo, shotguns, a scoped 30-06 Wheatherbee rifle, and enough ammo to start World War III.

Paul started the plan of approach with, "We'll go in about 0500 hours. If any neighbors happen to be awake they will just think we are going fishing. Most will be gone until next summer."

Fred added, "I know the neighborhood and they know me. I'll slip the shotgun into a fishing tube and walk into the back from a block away in case there is still someone at the lake. You be the diversion in the front, if needed. You enter after I'm in position behind the house." He didn't need a confirmation. Paul knew just what to do.

Where's the *Team*

The move to a dilapidated old house at the end of a dead-end road was not what the *Team* was used to. It stood inland a scant four miles from the Donner cottage on Lake Michigan. The Team was totally unaware they were so close to their prey.

Peeper expressed everyone's feelings, "It was all I could find in that time and at this late hour. At least it has heat! It's 1:00 A.M. and I'm beat. Let's find beds and talk in the morning."

Everyone quickly concurred. They set up surveillance equipment and guard duty. Beds, couches, anything they could lay on was where they crashed as Peeper took the first watch. They were taking a chance TQ was nowhere near. If they only knew TQ was so close! As it was, images of TQ stalking them with a myriad of weapons kept their sleep from being restful. Each member of the Team tossed in their sleep throughout the remainder of the night.

Scrambled eggs, toast, and coffee (lots of coffee) was the start of the day. Clean-up was completed by 0730. Spooky opened his first Lablatt Blue and banged it as a gavel on the kitchen table.

Spooky said, "We have to have someone in charge, to keep us together. It has to be someone we will all listen to. We need someone that isn't emotional. I nominate Toy. Anyone else want the responsibility?" He looked around. "No takers!" Spooky looked at each of the team, pausing to give the opportunity for a reply.

Toy confidently spoke, "I guess the silence is a consensus. If there were only one thing I learned about leadership from TQ, it's to listen to counsel then make the decision for action. No one here is the leader that TQ is. We all need to think and contribute. No more mistakes! We've had two mistakes already. What do you think about calling in some specialized outside help?"

Spooky declared, "No way! The Ghost has enemies that would be glad to help bring him down, but they may sense weakness in us as a team and take us all down. The less that know the better we all are."

Peeper countered with, "You are wrong man! Throw him to the wolves. Open his file and watch the fun from the safety of the bleachers. That ought to be some show!"

The discussion went back and forth for several hours and included a break for delivered pizza and beer.

Toy summarized this way, "Look... we haven't settled a thing. The arguments are all valid to some extent. If we keep after TQ, and failing, it will be the same as telling others we are weak and vulnerable. What if we tell just a few, those that have everything to lose if what we know about them gets to those that would love to see them dead. We'll say TQ took all our files to exchange for a clean slate. He knows governments and individuals that would want all of us dead. It would force those we select to join us... for as long as we need them. Then, we will off them at a farewell celebration."

Cypher declared, "That's what I'm talking about! We picked the right leader."

Three more hours of file searching for the most capable personnel to help with killing TQ narrowed the field down to four candidates. They were dubbed the FATAL FOUR. It would be fatal for TQ and the four candidates. Contacting them would not be too hard. Convincing them to help would be harder. They had to have the feeling they were about to be eliminated by an act of treachery by an operative they all knew and feared.

Time line to wrapping this up was two weeks from today.

Makes a real nice early Christmas present, Toy thought. She continued to make notes on the four persons they needed to join their team.

7
Coming Together

TQ's emotions were disorienting. A man known for his coolness and confidence, he was having a hard time thinking of anything but his current situation. Would the next few days bring enough peace, happiness, and friendship into TQ to change him forever? Like a well-worn cook book, the things he knew, the skills, were mentally shelved until needed. You can never discard completely the things which make you unique, different from everyone else. TQ is very unique!

TQ awoke with a start and quickly and immediately had it all together in his mind. It was 0458 hours! The couch was comfortable, but the sitting position was not. He went to get up and almost fell. His legs hanging down, crossed for hours, were still without feeling, he had no control of his muscles. His back was letting him know how bad it had been hurt as he stretched his large frame. Another person might have let out a groan or a hiss at the pain it brought. TQ allowed himself to squint his eyes and tighten his jaw. He thought of the way Anne returned his kisses and how she felt in his arms. It was almost as if she were still there. This was one of the most important things he had been missing his whole life... love, real love. Now it was his and nothing would be allowed to get in between him and Anne. Nothing!

The sudden appearance of a man of definite military bearing with a Glock pointed directly at him from the hallway had TQ looking for a weapon. The only thing he had was the pillow Anne had put under his head last night. All thought of fight stopped when the unmistakable feel of cold steel from twin shotgun barrels was pressed against the side of his head. He was effectively had. Something he heard or felt while sleeping must have awakened him. He hadn't recognized the danger until too late. He thought, *These guys are good, whoever they are.*

From the bedroom door Anne exclaimed, "Put up the hardware and grab some cups." She flipped on the lights and brushed Col. Stanton's gun up in the air, paused to give him a peck on the cheek, and headed for the little kitchen.

Anne looked at the uncomprehending men and said, "The coffee is old, but still warm. It might help take the chill out of this room. Dad, how about whipping up a huge breakfast, then we'll have introductions and explanations. I'm looking forward to some answers myself."

She thought to herself, *Maybe I'll get some insights about the man I fell in love with last night.*

The three men looked at each other with the baffled expressions of men who really didn't understand what had just happened and how this young woman just took over command of the whole situation. Obediently, the three men put away weapons, guns, and pillows. They reached for plates, utensils, and the makings of a breakfast only men of action, with adrenalin flowing, can devour.

Fred ordered TQ, "Hey you, get the grub out of the SUV!"

TQ dryly said, "Turner!"

Fred asked, "What?"

TQ answers, "Turner, that's my name."

Paul asks, "First or last?"

TQ returned, "First! Turner Quincy Freeman!"

Fred did the introductions. "I'm Fred Donner, Anne's father. That's Paul Stevens. He's Anne's godfather. He's an expert marksman."

Anne exclaimed with embarrassment, "Dad!"

Fred waved his hand and said, "Yeah, yeah, but if he doesn't hurry with getting the food I'll shoot him myself. I'm hungry!"

Anne exclaimed as she put together another pot of coffee, "Men!"

As he went for the sacks of groceries, TQ had a fleeting thought these two men were more than capable in the normal sense, but were not in his league. He could easily dispatch them and be gone, but so would any chance of a life with Anne. "Boy, look at these groceries! These guys like to eat as much as I do! I'm beginning to like these guys." TQ kicked the cottage door to get their attention. He stood in the light falling snow with his arms around four bags of groceries as Paul hurried to open the door.

TQ nodded toward the boat, "Nice boat."

Fred raised an eyebrow and asked, "You like to fish?"

TQ thought back through the years and replied pensively, "Did as a boy. Mountain Trout, light line, that's a great fight."

"Naw! It's the fight you get early in the morning from a big Bass," Paul retorted.

Fred jumped in with, "A good sized Perch or big Muskee is best!"

That was it! The challenge was down! The three men, and Anne, bantered lightly through the preparation, prayer, eating, and clean-up of breakfast like old friends brought together by a common pastime.

TQ felt at home. "Yeah! That's what it is! This is like the home, the people, I always wanted for a family – a family I never had." His heart ached to think he might lose it. When they heard about his past, what would they think? What would they do? What could he do about the *Team*? The *Team* didn't believe he just wanted to be done with it, to just walk away. If these people would have him, he would do whatever it took to keep his new family safe. In his mind, TQ said, *My family! Boy, am I getting way ahead of myself!*

He knew he had to tell them everything, to be honest, clean, and upfront. These two guys would be able to read a lie like a traffic signal on a clear night.

As Fred looked at TQ and Anne, Fred took control and ordered, "Everybody get coffee. I know there is something going on between you two. BUT! Now I need to know all about TQ. I think I can figure out some things from the name and happenings. However, I want it all or this situation is going to change fast! Who are you? Who are the creeps after you? Have you put my daughter in danger?"

Paul looked at his note pad and said, "I had pieces fitting together during breakfast. What I had come to me from my sources says you are a lot of trouble, a bomb about to go off in this kitchen. Great French toast by the way, TQ."

TQ nods his head, and smiles, "First time it's been edible."

Anne knew when to speak up and when to be quiet around men with large amounts of testosterone flowing. What she did, though, made all the difference, and gave TQ the hope and confidence to win over these stalwart men of great conviction. Anne simply picked up her chair and coffee cup opposite TQ and carried them to the other side of the table. She sat down next to TQ, looked her father and godfather in the eye, then turned to TQ.

Anne conveyed her confidence and loyalty by placing her hand on TQ's arm, saying simply, "I'm ready to hear it all, the good and the bad."

TQ stared at his coffee cup while drawing several deep breaths. Where should he start? He turned and looked into Anne's eyes and started. He began when he was a boy on the reservation, after he lost his parents. His mother died of a sickness when he was a toddler. He thought it was cancer, but was unsure. He was never told. His father went hunting in the mountains on the reservation when TQ was ten and never returned. He had fallen to his death. His grandfather became his everything. He taught TQ the old ways of courage, honesty, honor, to know one's enemies, the code of a warrior, and loyalty to family and friends. In his own way, he lavished TQ with tough, but gentle, love. TQ mentioned his one year of college at Arizona State. The turning point in his life came when he joined the Army after his money for college ran out. The military lured him with promises and half truths about who the real enemy was, how his skills would make all the difference to the free world. The change in his life came with the deception of federal agents recruiting a young man of less than twenty years. They wanted the use of his natural talents and abilities, fine-tuned by an aged grandfather from a nobler generation. They succeeded in turning him into a killing machine that didn't question their motives! The government, hiding behind a cloak of righteous indignation at similar actions from other countries, deceived one of their best. The formation of the *Team* was next. Though young, as a capable leader, TQ had a major part in putting the *Team* together.

Occasionally Paul would interject comments like, "It figures. That sounds about right."

Out loud Fred would just remark, "Buttheads!" Under his breath were several expletive words he didn't use in mixed company.

Anne stared intently at TQ and wiped away a stray tear from her eyes now and then. The womanly compassion for the man she loved coming to the surface. The strength of her character making her steadfast in the confidence she had that God didn't make mistakes. He brought TQ to her for life.

It was a lot of information. It was hard for TQ to bring it out, to put it under a microscope for the people he had just met, or anybody, for that matter. The telling passed through lunch, a pot of coffee, and several afternoon beers each when Fred halted the conversations.

Fred loudly exclaimed, "Enough! This tale sounds like a mystery writer going off the deep end!"

Paul countered, "Yeah, but it rings all too true. Remember what I told you about how the Feds approached me after 'Nam? I believe him. Listen!

Don't give us names, dates, places, or how you did your job. No details! You would only put all of us in jeopardy. What are your plans now?"

Before he could stop himself, TQ blurted out, "I want to marry, have three kids, and be a fishing guide on a big lake somewhere where I can enjoy a quiet life with my family."

Anne just got red in the face and smiled to herself.

Fred asked, "We get to fish free, right?"

They all laughed when TQ exclaimed, "Only if you make breakfast and Paul drives the boat. From what Ann tells me, I'd be living dangerously with you piloting the boat."

When the laughter died, Anne demanded, "Hey, what do I get to do in all this?"

TQ turned fully around toward Anne and his face took on a seriousness which belied his nervousness. He paused until the men squirmed and Anne felt like she couldn't breathe. Then, he quietly and firmly announced, "Why, you'll cook for and clean up after our three beautiful children. Together we will raise them, our family."

Anne spoke as her heart fairly thumped out of her chest, "Only three?"

Anne and TQ sat and stared at each other, eyes locked, silently speaking askance, acceptance, love, and commitment while their fingers found each other and firmly held tight.

Paul and Fred sat staring; first at each other and then the young couple in quiet disbelief. Sure, they liked this guy, even trusted him for an unknown reason, but Anne marrying him… Whoa! Their eye contact conveyed their mutual thoughts:

Can we stop it? Probably not!

Can we help him get out of his old life? Don't know, but we are going to try.

Someone may get hurt! Yeah, but we are going to do it for Anne.

The two old friends, warriors together, knew without speaking these things. They just nodded to each other. Fred began to clean the table as his eyes moistened, remembering his wife, Anne's mother.

After a long 30 seconds of silent communication, Anne announced, "Well, you men better get ready for some afternoon fishing. You are on your own for supper. I have shopping to do. Thanksgiving is two days away."

In what sounded like surround sound, the three startled men echoed, "What shopping?"

Anne replied, "We certainly aren't going back to the house. Sooo, I have to get a turkey, all the trimmings, and enough stuff to make a couple of pumpkin pies."

TQ responded, "Deep dish apple pie!"

Anne said, "With French vanilla ice cream for al-a-mode. You guys go fish and make your plans. I've got to get ready to feed you three a Thanksgiving meal you will never forget. Remember! You are on your own for supper."

Fred threw out, "Chicken and dumplings is good on a cold, damp day like this. I make great chicken and dumplings."

Paul added, "Lots of coffee, black and high test."

TQ reiterated, "And deep-dish apple pie!"

Fred glanced from TQ to Anne and said, "Well, at least he isn't hard to please."

Outside, the two older men flanked TQ as they headed for the boat and an afternoon of fishing and planning.

8
Fateful Encounter

Spooky, Crimp, and Cypher were roaming the local supermarket buying food and beer to last at least a week. Spooky was a good cook, but Cypher was an exceptional baker. As the others left the produce and headed for the meat aisle, Cypher turned into the baking aisle. He always checked for new, free recipes. He almost bumped into the beautiful strawberry blonde reading the back of a can of apple pie filling.

Cypher hurriedly exclaimed, "Uhhh! Sorry lady!"

Anne smiled and said, "That's ok. I was just trying to find a recipe for deep dish apple pie. I've never made one and I have a special request for the holiday from a guest."

Cypher excitedly expressed, "Hey, that's my specialty!"

Anne, with a slightly raised eyebrow, exclaimed with a hint of sarcasm, "Yeah, sure it is!"

As if trying to exonerate himself, Cypher exclaimed, "No kidding! You have a paper and something to write with. I'll write it down for you. Don't use this stuff. Use fresh baking apples! Go with Macintosh or Granny Smith. Leave the skin on and the macs will give the pie a pretty pink color."

Anne handed him the items from her purse and waited as he wrote down the ingredients and explained the process.

Just as they finished, Spooky popped around the corner and said to Cypher, "Knew you would be here. We need help with loading the bags a least. Come on!"

Cypher answered, "Right with you!" To Anne he said, "Remember, if it is for a man, cover it with a crust and put lots of cinnamon and sugar on it. It'll be a big hit if you cut his initials in the crust."

Anne replied, "Thanks! I'll try it."

She finished her shopping, two carts full, and headed back to the cottage on the lake. It was going to be a great thanksgiving. She was determined to start immediately making fancy relishes and appetizers.

9
Thinking Ahead

Special Agent Katherine Scott had never heard of their agency working so closely with a military agency. This Col. Stanton was in charge and she was in the dark!

Special Agent (SA) Scott was a good agent because she was never in the dark for long. Her orders were to aid in every way. No one had said she couldn't snoop. That was her job!

She rapidly searched for any information about the Colonel and the case at hand. At every turn, her access was denied! Who is this handsome Colonel and what was he working on? She didn't realize she had the word handsome in her thoughts as she pictured him staring after her at the airport as she drove off.

It had been almost two years since her last personal relationship ended in disaster. She had sworn not to jump into another relationship, but she remembered the extremely male way the Colonel stared at her. It was like he couldn't help himself. It made her feel good again. She thought, *Nuts! I'm not going there.* Still, she had his cell number and the SUV was a GM product. *Hummmm, that thing has on-star and I have the plate number,* Katherine thought out loud. It was just that easy to call the on-star operator and explain her husband had gone to the lake fishing and she had to locate him for a family emergency. It would only be an hour and twenty-minute drive from where she was now. Why would she go? Why, to assist, make sure he had the right weapons, food, and an opportunity to get acquainted. Pack tonight and leave at 0700 hours in the morning. Better take all the appropriate clothing. She smiled to herself and thought, *Maybe I should pack something a little tighter for dining out on the holiday.*

The only family she had was a younger sister in Paduka, Kentucky. They only saw each other every couple of years at best. They loved each other, but her job and life made a distance between them that was more than geography. There was really no place for her to be for the holidays. Maybe, just maybe, there would be a special place to be this year.

10

The Team Expands

As our three shoppers returned, Toy expressed some frustration: "You guys took long enough. Get everything we need? Peck is coming in two days. I invited him for the holiday. After I explained how his life might end soon, he was glad to be here, with precautions, of course. That's Peck!"

Spooky said defensively, "We'd have been here a half hour ago, but Cypher was giving some chick cooking lessons."

Cypher throws his hands in the air and says, "Hey, she needed expert help and, TA DA, there I was! Besides, it was baking lessons; a far superior endeavor than loading shopping carts."

Ricco asks, "You get her number or address?"

Cypher replied, "Naw! I was rushed out of the store by the goon squad here."

Crimp laughed and said, "No matter. She was out of your league anyway. She was a lady!"

Cypher retorted, "Ha, when was the last time you even talked to a woman."

Toy demanded, "What am I, chopped liver?"

Cypher shrugged and replied, "I guess I just think of you as one of the guys."

Toy threw back, "I'm flattered, I think. Let's put this stuff away and try to find the other three."

Tuesday in Paris

Manny Peck was on a bench basking in the late autumn sun and feeding the pigeons by the Seine River when he received the call from Toy. He took the call then checked out the info she fed him. It had the smell of trouble. Hell, any time anybody went against TQ Freeman it meant trouble! Manny wasn't the least bit afraid. When he called Toy back, he was already on his way to the airport. Manny was a man of action. It was time to get into action. No matter the outcome, Manny would face whatever was coming his way head-on.

It didn't fit, TQ turning them all over like that. Manny would keep his eye on Toy and the rest of TQ's old friends. Toy expected him tomorrow. He'd be there today to look around. It was always best to know as much or more than enemies or so-called friends who could become enemies.

Wednesday in Illinois

Like most people in the business, Rosalita DeJesus had no family. B. J. Wentzel, the opposite, and an exception in the business, doted on his family. Both were arriving today.

"Better than eating alone", B.J. commented to himself as he waited at O'Hara for Peeper to pick him up. He was thinking of the holiday and family he would be missing.

Rosalita came in from Puerto Rico a half hour earlier and was explaining to a new bride what to cook to keep her new husband happy at home. B.J. sat down in the big chair across from her. Though they had never met, they exchanged knowing nods and became absorbed in their own business while waiting. Tomorrow's holiday would be a good day of relaxation before getting down to the business of killing that rat T.Q. Freeman. Give them up for amnesty, NOT!

Toy made it clear all their lives were in the toilet if TQ got away with all the files he had.

Manny watched Peeper help load up two new members to the team at the airport. He would give them time to get where they were going and call to have someone come back for him. He didn't like the way this felt. It just wasn't right – not the way covert teams operated. How many were on the original *Team* TQ had put together? Now there were two more, plus him! He hadn't met the two, but he knew them from his own files. What's the deal? He was known as a loner, and this was getting very crowded. About that time, a woman in a grey business suit and shoulder length auburn hair gave him a look he couldn't neglect. He followed her to a table in the nearest bar. At least the wait would be pleasant.

The last member of the "*Fatal Four*" was due in the day after Thanksgiving. He was flying into Buffalo, New York. There he was picking up a special vehicle and driving to Chicago. Someone would meet him at a truck stop on the highway and lead him back to the safehouse.

11
Planning At The Lake

Fred, Paul and TQ had fished all day Tuesday. They caught 14 fish and threw them back. They had developed almost as many plans of action and threw them all out, too. Just when they thought they had it nailed down, more information about TQ, or the team, would surface and quickly negate the plan. It was discouraging to think of what they were up against, but there was no quit in them. They talked after supper until late in the evening with no success.

Now, the smell of coffee, eggs, and ham brought all the men to the kitchen for breakfast. It struck TQ the men all got up early, but Anne was up far enough ahead of them to have their breakfast ready. He was both amazed and smugly pleased, but didn't know why he should be. Actually, he felt pride in Anne he had for no one else.

Anne turned from flipping pancakes, "TQ, you know what the team's strengths are. Do you realize you are their one weakness, now that you are not there! You took all those talents, if you will, and used them to mold the *Team* together. Who will they pick to replace you? It certainly won't be someone from outside. How will that new leader think? What drives that person? That is your key."

The three veteran warriors sat and stared at the beautiful rookie cop in the blue and white checkered apron with humility and a new appreciation until Anne uncomfortably exclaimed, "Well, what?"

Paul exclaimed, "That's it! TQ's loss is the key to their defeat."

TQ with disbelief answers, "We always discussed the plans as a *Team*."

Fred replied, "Yeah, but who put all the ideas together and made them work?"

TQ hesitantly stated in a flat tone, "Well, I guess I did."

Anne said with satisfaction, "See, I had it right! I just knew you were the key."

Paul asks, "Think, TQ, who would take over? Is there anyone strong enough to just take the position against any opposition? How will the position be filled? Is there more than one that would vie for the position, causing strife within the ranks?"

Fred cautioned, "Slow down, Paul. Let him think. Anne, you did well. How about refills on the coffee."

Anne pointedly states, "How about breakfast? It's hot and ready, now. Talk later!"

Breakfast was a quiet affair, with an occasional bit of info provided by TQ. Paul quickly added it to a growing file of information on a yellow legal pad. Between first and second helpings, Paul turned on his cell phone. He had to contact Special Agent Katherine, somebody to do legwork, maybe get an artist to make some sketches of the *Team* since there were no pictures of the *Team*. It was no sooner on than it was ringing.

Paul gruffly spoke into his cell. "Paul Stanton here, who's this?"

Katherine informed him, "This is Special Agent Scott. I've been trying to locate you all last night and this morning. What's happening?"

Paul asked, "Special Agent who?"

Katherine exclaimed rather loudly, "Katherine!"

Paul replied with, "Oh, sorry, I didn't have your last name. Do you have paper and something to write with? There are things I want you to do, necessary supplies to get, and locate a sketch artist."

There was a slight pause while Katherine got a pad and pen to make the list.

Returning to the phone, Katherine threw out, "Fire away!"

After giving her a lengthy list, Paul asked her, "You get all that?"

Katherine replied, "Sure! How do I get it to you?"

Paul gives her directions. "Rent a car through the office channels. Don't use your own. Get everything together. Don't forget to find an artist that's single. Make it look like a date to an outsider. These guys have connections. Follow the directions I've given to you to the marina. If it's safe we'll contact you about 15 minutes after you arrive. What? Yes, sit close to the guy. You're supposed to be on a date, remember. If we don't come to get you within twenty-five minutes of your arrival at the pier, something is wrong. Make like you're having a fight in and out of the car. Demand to be taken home and do it. I'll contact you secure two hours after you leave, if that's the case. Thanksgiving dinner! Yes, certainly, if you are here you will both eat with us. Bring nothing, we have plenty. See you at 1600 hours, plus or minus five ticks."

12
Science Catches Up

Back at the Police Academy

Doc Bailey was very thorough. While he cleaned TQ's wounds, he had put away several tissue and blood samples. He heard Fred Donner and his daughter had hastily requested leave and it didn't add up. A call to his old friend, Pete, at Chicago CSI and the samples went off for rush DNA testing. That was yesterday. Pete was on his home phone this Wednesday morning with hushed excitement in his voice.

Doc Bailey chided his friend, "Pete, slow down. I can't understand a thing you're saying. Who's dead? What dead man? Stop the riddles! Turner Quincy Freeman! Dead for how long? You sure you tested my stuff? Three times! You haven't mentioned this to anyone, not anyone at all, have you? Good! Don't! Go back, now, right now! Destroy all the test matter, samples, paperwork, results, everything. Bring one copy of the info to me in an hour. We'll meet at the McDonalds in the WALMART on your side of town. Right! Now go, for God's sake! Lives may depend on it, even ours."

Doc grabbed his hat and coat, kissed his wife and merely said, "Have to see to a patient. I'll be back as soon as I can."

McDonalds was crowded. The meeting of two old friends was very smooth. Pete fell right into the moment and had purchased an extra-large card for an old friend. It was a card the folded reports would fit into nicely. A cup of coffee, some conversation about the families, wishing happy Thanksgiving, and a cordial goodbye and they parted company. It all took twelve minutes.

Doc made a quick stop at the office to pull Fred's cell phone number from the call out sheet. At 1030, he had Fred's cell phone ringing.

The four were still around the table trying to plan and alternate plan for possible events. The call was not expected. They all looked at Fred and the cell phone as he hesitantly answered it.

Fred answers the phone, "Donner here. Oh, Doc! Sure, I can talk, what's up? Yeah, I know the guy. He's been dead how long? Well, your dead guy ate six pancakes, four eggs, and two slices of ham. Whoops, Anne says three slices of ham with toast and coffee for breakfast this morning. Yes, I know all about him. We've been having a lot of discussions the last two days. Say, you keep that phone charged and handy. I may need your skills. No, I'm not sick, but I'm thinking there may be an illness brewing here. Call you in the next day or so." Fred sat back in the kitchen chair with a widening of the eyes, a raised brow, and the trace of a smile turning up the corners of his mouth.

Paul flatly states, "I've seen that look before. What are you up to?"

Fred, frowning a little, replied, "I'm not sure yet. Let it simmer awhile. We need to figure out who is in charge of that team and the direction it may lead them. Hopefully that direction isn't here."

Anne recapped their discussion, "We've got it down to two, Spooky and Toy. Why use all the nicknames?"

TQ answered, "Doesn't give up our real names. What's this about my breakfast?"

Fred replied, "Doc, the guy that patched you up, took samples of your body and ran DNA tests on them against all available banks. You are who you say you are. That's a comfort, I guess. BUT, and I say BUT, you died at age twenty-three! You don't look bad for a dead guy."

TQ sighed and said, "Modern science catches up! It's harder to trace a dead man that travels light. The government took care of that for everyone on the team, all teams. We are not the only team. Each person died in such a way that no one would even think to challenge the death certificate. In some cases, there were even unknown bodies to put in caskets. A few of the caskets just had sand bags in them. Mine was one with sandbags. I guess they couldn't find a dead Indian."

"We have to stop being the hunted and hunt them to survive, or run and hide forever. I won't do that, now that I've met Anne."

Paul states a bit stiffly, "Yeah, but the price of a hunt for that pack of animals will cost some, maybe all, our lives. Then what do you have?"

TQ responded, "Sorry, I'm not used to thinking about family."

Anne smiled and said, "That has a nice sound, family." She stepped behind TQ and put both of her hands on his broad shoulders.

Fred chided TQ, "Boy, her mom had that same look for me. You're done! Your goose is cooked for sure."

Seriously TQ replied, "I'd want nothing else. Fred, this is fast, I know. When we get out of this mess, can I have permission to seek your daughter's hand in marriage?"

Anne clapped her hands together and exclaimed, "Yes! Yes!"

Fred raises his right eyebrow and asks Paul, "Paul, is my voice getting higher?"

Paul answered, "Must be!" He turned to TQ, "Boy you got a god-father to consider, too. I take it real serious."

Anne looked at her god father and wrinkled her nose. Then she turned to TQ and blurted, "He says yes, too, TQ."

13
Reinforcements

Katherine hung up the phone, stood up, and started talking to herself, "He wants me to come for Thanksgiving dinner with his friends. Snap out of it. This is just business. I'd better get to the office. First, call Jim Frey and tell him he is on duty for Thanksgiving dinner. Rent a car, get maps, contact the US Marshals, brief the Regional Director, and pick up a nice bottle of white wine to go with a turkey dinner. I must remember to tell Jim to bring his sketching pads and stuff."

O'Hare Airport, Chicago

Manny made the call to the *Team* to pick him up at the airport after four drinks and a light lunch with Ms. Ainsworth. Lunch netted a telephone number and a date in late December in New York City.

Ricco answered the cell phone, "Hello."

Manny asked Ricco, "This is Manny. I'm at the airport. Is someone picking me up and taking me to my hotel, or do I rent a Lexus SUV from here?"

Ricco caustically interjected, "Nice to hear from you, too, old friend."

Manny calmly replied, "I'm not your old friend. I'm not your new friend. I don't like you. This is business. Give me someone that knows what's going on."

Ricco tosses the phone to Toy, "Toy, an old friend wants to chat."

Toy, all business, speaks into the cell phone she deftly caught, "Toy here!"

Without identifying himself, Manny asked, "Someone taking me to my hotel or do I rent a vehicle?"

Toy replied with a suggestive tone, "We thought you should stay here with the rest of us."

Emphatically, Manny stated, "Wrong thought! I'll help plan. I'll do what's needed, but I'm not part of your evil little group. This is strictly self-preservation for me. When we are done, I'm gone, fast."

Toy replied in a flat, slightly irritated tone, "Do what you want. Peeper will meet you in front of your hotel tomorrow to show you the way here. Call between 0600 and 0700. We're having a holiday meal. You're welcome to enjoy it with us."

"I have a hotel reservation anyway. See you in the AM." Manny abruptly replied and just as abruptly hung up the phone. Manny left the airport in the Lexus he had reserved from Paris the day before. He always planned one step ahead of others. It kept him alive. The suite in a five-star hotel was his idea of a safe house. They provide excellent security. He knew it wouldn't take Cypher long to find out where he was staying, so there was no need for him to tell them where to meet him in the morning. His profession provided for all his wants, needs, and an ever-increasing nest egg. Like TQ, he planned for the future; an uncertain future, but it was all he had to look forward to. At this point, Manny didn't think about retirement, it was totally foreign. Today was his first and only thoughts of getting out of this life.

Manny mulled over his life to date. Every time you did a job, you acquired knowledge which could potentially hurt someone. If that someone started to worry about you, you could be elevated to the top of a hit list yourself. It might be time to change careers. Maybe, sell used cars. Nah, nothing that dishonest! Maybe something in the country, up in the mountains where there's solitude and time to read. Let the wolves fight among themselves!

The valet accepted the twenty-dollar bill Manny handed him along with the keys to the Lexus and promised to back the car into a space on the ground level within five spaces of the exit. The valet said he would bring the keys up to the gentleman's room before he could unpack.

The valet identified himself, "Name's Dino. Room 1605! Might I suggest a move to 1611 or 1612? They are very close to the stairs, for the man that likes to be prepared for an emergency!"

Manny looked at him in silence for a full ten seconds. The valet looked back.

Manny asked, "I would remember you if we met somewhere."

Dino replied, "No sir, you don't know me. My parents died before I knew why. Drugs! I was raised by my grandparents. Mostly though, I was raised on the street, by street people. I keep my mouth shut, watch and listen. Learned to read people, who to help and who to stay away from!"

"Think you have my story in less than two minutes, huh?" Manny challenged.

Dino flippantly replied, "Pretty much. No details though."

Manny dismissed him with, "I'm waiting and so is my room."

Dino holds up a hand and dials the front desk, "Just a minute. Hey! Bobby, my man! I thought you were on reservations tonight! You have a room on the 16th floor for a Mr." (Pause and a raised eyebrow.)

Manny's curt response was, "Peck!"

Dino returned to Bobby on the phone: "Peck, Mr. Peck. Yeah, that's the one. Listen, he needs to be in 1612." Silence while they waited on Bobby. Yeah, I knew you could make it happen. No, it's personal. Nothing across the hand! Just you and me! Remember the redhead I introduced you to last Saturday night? Thanks! We're even, Bobby."

Manny said with respect, "Even I had to take the room they offered because of the holiday. You pick up a phone and make this happen in just about a minute and a half. I'm impressed!"

Dino hands back the twenty and offers Manny his services with, "Mr. Peck, anything you want, except drugs. You understand!"

Manny shook his hand and replaced the twenty with a "C" note in one smooth movement.

Dino said, "Name's Dino Pachelli. Got plenty of green! I can always use a friend." He took out a pen, wrote on the "C" note, and handed it back. "Put this phone number on your voice dialer. Your room is waiting."

Manny had turned to leave when Dino's voice stopped him.

Dino asked, "Mr. Peck, you like to read? I figure you to be educated. My office is the library two blocks down, second floor, biographies of famous people. You can learn a lot from dead people!"

Manny watchfully replied, "From live ones, too!" Then, he turned and took the stairs, not the elevator, to the sixteenth floor, two steps at a time. It was his way to get cardio exercise on a tight schedule. Using every minute efficiently is his way of life.

Six minutes later, Manny tipped the bellboy and unpacked three thousand-dollar suits and Italian shoes. Manny enjoyed the good life. Tonight, he was going to forego his desire to taste Chicago's night life. He had to concentrate on this drive by TQ's old Team to eliminate TQ. The story of TQ's treachery was possible, but highly improbable from all he knew and had pieced together over the last few years. He was waiting on street talk even now, waiting for tips. There are people in this world who survive by knowing everyone else's business. Chicago had its share. Manny had contacts lots of places, Chicago was no exception. He thought, *Let's see what turns up! That kid, Dino, he might be useful.* Manny's knitted brow gave away his pensive thought process.

14
Puzzle Pieces

Meanwhile, the *Team* plus two of the *"Fatal Four"* were running through scenarios, trying to figure out tactics TQ employed in disappearing, again, like a ghost.

He appeared to be hurt badly by the bomb.

He would need more medical attention.

TQ hadn't shown up at any of the places that took care of the underground medical needs of friend and foe.

He vanished out of a clinic crawling with cops.

There had been no movement to known safe houses.

There were no known attempts of injured people his size to use public transportation.

No one of his description or known disguises rented any vehicles.

TQ had a strict code against stealing from the common man. He would say, "Someone worked hard for that. I'll not take it from them!" A stolen vehicle, though possible, was probably out of the question.

They agreed their conclusions were sound:

TQ was still out there somewhere!

He had help, maybe lots of it.

He still might be at the police academy, but doubtful.

TQ probably is where he has medical help for his wounds.

He is laying low until his wounds heal.

When TQ is healed he will need weapons to come after them.

TQ will come after them!

In the Hotel Parking Garage

Dino hadn't been totally honest with Manny. He sat in Manny's rented Lexus, with a notebook and pen, making calls and making brief notes from the info which had just flowed back to him from the street. This Peck wasn't a wise guy, more likely a private soldier. He definitely was not one to make mad. How did he fit into the mystery of the disappearing man from the Police Academy? The street was humming about this guy. Hurt in a car bomb blast, the guy vaporizes in a clinic surrounded by cops. There was no reason Dino could verify, but it was a sure thing Mr. Peck was involved. Maybe he was government, but whose? Not much information after all the calls Dino made. Even though he liked Peck, he would get no help from Dino if he found out Peck was from another government. There was a lot of whispering going around, like the sound leaves make before a violent storm. There had to be a key to make sense of all the bits of information out there.

Dino exclaimed aloud to himself, "Keys! Crap, Peck might need them. Sixteenth floor here I come." His feeling of urgency forced him to take the stairs three at a time.

FBI Headquarters, Chicago

Jim Frey left the FBI office, picked up the rental, and drove the eighteen blocks to get Special Agent Scott at her downtown apartment.

She gave him a quick peck on the cheek and whispered, "We're supposed to be lovers, but you keep your hands to yourself." Jim smiled a roguish smile, grabbed the bouquet of flowers from off the front seat, and waved them in the air like a pirate with a sword, then gently held them out to her. Katherine grinned, in spite of herself.

The ice was broken. Anyone watching would have believed the illusion. No one was watching.

During the drive to the marina, Katherine briefed Jim on the case as she knew it. Jim usually sat in an office waiting for requests for his skills as an artist to sketch people involved in a case. This was Jim's first case in the field and he was excited. It must be important to have him leave his office. He and Special Agent Scott had to look legitimate as a couple. Scott was doing her part by sitting close.

Frey dubiously stated, "I hope my Fiancée's friends don't see this. I won't be able to explain it to her satisfaction."

Scott says, with an apology, "I'm sorry. I thought you were unattached or I would have gotten someone else. You are the best artist in the district office! I naturally sought you."

Jim Frey couldn't help swell a little with pride at her words.

Frey responded with, "No, I'm glad to be a part of the case. I'll be glad to help anyway I can. By the way, you haven't told me much about it. I heard you were talking to the US Marshal's office, too. How big is this?"

Scott came back with, "I don't know how big it is, but I know it's dangerous. It has the possibility of a lot of collateral damage. You heard about that mystery man who disappeared out of the Chicago Police Academy clinic? Well, all I know is it involves him. This Colonel from the Army CID is in charge. It is really mixed up. That's all I know."

Jim responded to the information with an update of his own, "Ok! We're close to the marina now. We'll probably be briefed in depth within the hour."

Jim turned into the marina and looked for the parking place where they were to wait for their contact. The parking place, near the pier, provided the classic scene of buildings, dreary weather, water, boats, and men too stubborn to give up on fishing, even in nasty weather. There were three middle aged men and one old man with white hair sticking out from under a Cubs baseball cap. He was collecting his bait bucket and rod. The scarf around his nose and mouth protected him from the cold wind of a November afternoon blowing off the lake.

As he slowly walked past their car, the rod slipped from his hand and struck the driver side door. He motioned for Jim to roll down his window. Then he stuck his hand in toward Jim as he apologized for the rod striking the car. Jim was explaining it would be OK, the car was a rental. He felt the folded paper being slipped into his hand. He almost showed his surprise, but waved with his left hand and gave the correct response, "Don't worry about it. It'll all work out." The old fisherman shuffled off toward the cottages down the street. The two agents sat enjoying what was left of the sunset, acutely aware of the note tucked safely between them. At the sun's last light, Jim started the car, turned on the lights, and left the pier. Special Agent Scott unfolded a map and hid the note inside. Jim politely turned on the interior light, like any nice date would have done.

Special Agent Scott read the note aloud while hiding her face behind the map, excitement mounting in her voice. "Here are the directions to where we are to meet. Go down two streets, turn left. Go three blocks, turn left, then, left again. Next, turn into the driveway of cottage 61. Drive straight across the yard to the garage of the cottage behind it. This is the driveway. Turn here! That must be the one right there. There's the old fisherman pointing to the open garage door. Drive in!"

The door shut, but no lights came on. A red chemical Light came to life, subdued by the cloth wrapped around it. The light was held close to the floor. Its movement summoned them to get out of the car and to follow the old fisherman. The voice of the old fisherman turned suddenly into the strong tones of Colonel Stanton, tones which immediately upset Katherine Scott's thought process. Jim was nudging her with his elbow.

Jim whispered hoarsely, "Hey, let's go! Get your bag. I'm not your boyfriend anymore."

Katherine retrieved her bag and followed the shadows, which were the two men, through the less dark doorway into the cottage. The ceiling light came on and revealed two more men and a beautiful young woman she didn't know in a small, but tidy, kitchen.

Colonel Stanton provided introductions as he removed his hat and makeup.

Did she want to see that, or did he really pause for a second to scan her with his eyes. Katherine couldn't help smiling. This time, as Col. Stanton returned his gaze to Katherine, he did pause, just a second or two, and smiled back.

Paul completed the introductions with, "And last, this is Turner Quincy Freeman. TQ, the man all this fuss is about. First, we'll have some supper. We'll brief you when you are settled in. I'm in with Fred. Katie, err Katherine, can stay in the other bedroom with Anne. Jim and Katherine have rooms at the motel, but they should opt to stay here tonight since it will be late when we are done talking. Jim and TQ bunk on the living room couch or cot. You two decide who gets what. Beauty and age both have it over you guys."

TQ nodded.

Jim shrugged and said, "I can sleep anywhere."

Anne was just finishing setting the table with TQ's help when Katherine entered. She had changed into beige slacks and a maroon top that complimented her skin and hair. Katherine was followed closely by Paul, who had just come in from the garage. He was watching Katherine and successfully tuning out Jim Frey's questions.

Paul, with an apology in his voice said, "What? Sorry Jim, my mind was somewhere else."

TQ caught Anne's eye and winked just once.

Anne couldn't help herself. She broke into a girlish giggle just thinking about her godfather being smitten like that. She thought, *Men, they never grow up. There is always a young man in there somewhere. At least, that's what every woman hopes for.*

Fred set the tone for the meal: "First, we pray. Then, we eat. No talking business! We need to get to know each other personally. That way we'll make fewer mistakes when we do talk business. You can ask business questions when the meal is over. Clear? Good! Let's pray!"

At the Hotel

Manny mused about the information, pieces not completely fitting, his sources and Dino supplied. He patted the Sig 40 beneath his left arm, almost affectionately. He thought how Dino had filled this request in less than fifty minutes. The price seemed a little steep. The kid explained the gun was clean and it came with two advantages. It was then Dino held out the two military frag grenades.

Dino bluntly stated, "These will even the odds if needed."

15
Thanksgiving

The Team

Manny followed Peeper to the safe house the next morning. Forty-two and a half minutes at the speed limit. Not far from the lake, either. He would have to talk to Dino about that. Another minute and he was greeted by TQ's old *Team* like long lost friends. Definitely a put on! There was hostility from old wounds not far under the surface. He could feel it, especially from Ricco. Manny thought, *Don't ever let that one get behind you, Manny. Play along. Let them think all's well and get the full story. Toy is in charge. Good choice!* Her one weakness… she thinks all men melt at her charms. Well, it might be nice to play along there, too. He gave her a smile and a candid once over. She smiled and openly looked back.

Toy handed him a sheaf of notes across the table and said, "Its thanksgiving. You can read over these while we set up the big meal. I just love holidays, don't you?"

Manny replied, "I'm not much for crowds. Two people make a great holiday, I'd say."

Toy smiled in a matter-of-fact way, "I'd like to try that some time."

"Yes, sir," Manny thought. "She is very sure of herself."

The others grabbed drinks, some appetizers, and slid into whatever seats they could grab to watch the football games on TV. Manny read the notes Toy gave him and sipped slowly on brandy from the bottle and glass he brought with him. Still, he was listening to the banter, the cheers, and the off-hand comments about TQ. Mentally he organized the pieces to add to those already in order. By the time the first game was over, the comments had begun to rerun like tired old shows on syndicated television. Manny got up in the middle of his third brandy and offered his assistance to Toy in setting the table. Rose and Cypher were put the finishing touches on the meal preparations. It all smelled great! It had been a long time since he sat down to a holiday meal with any kind of group. Mostly, holidays had been meals alone in the room of a five-star hotel somewhere. He felt an urge to let go, to join in the festive mood of the group. Then, he surveyed who was here and what it was about. That was enough to put a damper on his festive mood!

Manny said to himself, "Don't trust any of them Manny; especially this woman smiling at you with the come-on in her eyes. If she were a man, I think I'd almost be afraid of her. Heck, I am afraid of her!"

Instead, Manny smiled grandly and thanked Toy for insisting he come over for dinner and the company.

Toy asked, "Which is better, the dinner or the company?"

Manny threw a glance at the bountiful table. Then, slowly, ran his eyes down and up Toy's figure. He just grinned crookedly and said, "Time will tell, I hope."

Toy looked at the frame of this handsome man and softly said, "Everyone should have a wish come true during the holidays."

Cypher hollered over the TVs loud volume, "Foods hot and available. Turn up the game a little more and get to the table. Hey, I'm a poet! Rosalita and I outdid ourselves on this one."

As one, the group moved to the table. Toy took a place at one end and Manny, naturally, took the chair at the other end. No one seemed to notice, except Spooky. Being second was no problem, but he had somehow assumed the chair Manny was in belonged to him. Seeds of discord, envy, and bitterness were firmly planted in Spooky's heart.

The meal was attacked with gusto. The lighthearted banter around the table belied the undercurrent of distrust and the basic ruthlessness TQ was trying to leave behind. Manny was the only one aware of the level these human spirits were sinking to. It wasn't a conscious realization, just a subtle awareness. It was not how he wanted to be.

Ricco raised his voice over the others, "Hey, I'm ready for dessert!"

Toy had the feeling she wasn't leading the team like TQ. They weren't anticipating what needed to be done. She was a good leader, but TQ was extraordinary! TQ had something you couldn't put your finger on. That something was the difference between good leaders and great leaders. It was the difference between her and TQ. It seemed he asked questions to see if the *Team* could come up with the correct answers. They were answers he already possessed.

The football game ended a few minutes before the meal was over. Toy turned off the TV. She ordered the table cleared of the plastic plates and flatware, leftovers, and empty beer bottles. The party was over.

At the Lake
Thanksgiving breakfast was early and quick. Anne declared the kitchen a *woman's domain* as they had a ton of food to prepare. The men had to get out of the way!

Armed with coffee cups, jackets, and gloves, the men went out to prepare the boat for one last fishing trip, if the weather held. It didn't look good. They wouldn't get much fishing done. Mostly, it would be planning and trying to figure out what the *Team* was going to do next.

Anne asked TQ, "Aren't you forgetting something, TQ?"

Puzzled, TQ simply asked her, "What?"

Anne, with no hint of shyness stated, "It's an old family tradition that the men never leave the house without giving their women a goodbye kiss!"

TQ scooped her up into the air by the waist like a little child. Smiling broadly, he exclaimed, "I love traditions!"

He gave her a long tender kiss before setting her, somewhat breathless, back on her feet. Then he left the cottage at a run to catch up with the other men.

Katherine softly said to Anne, "I've been waiting for that all my life!"

Anne hooked her arm in Katherine's and said, "I've seen how my god-father looks at you. I like you. How would you like to be my god-mother?"

Katherine frowned and said, "UUUGH! That makes me sound so old!"

Anne cocked her head to one side and states, "Well, you didn't answer my question!"

Katherine candidly replied, "I won't say I'm not attracted, but it's too early to tell."

Anne pensively states, "Is it? I wonder."

With mock admonishment, Katherine states, "Enough young lady! I do a great turkey and stuffing!"

Anne zealously exclaimed, "Awesome! I'll do pies, relishes, and start the mashed potatoes. Nothing but real mashed potatoes is allowed in this house!"

Katherine proved good to her word with the turkey. Anne applied her mom's recipe to the pumpkin pie. The newly acquired recipe from the friendly man at the supermarket became a ten-inch, deep dish apple pie. Before Anne put it in the oven to bake, she carefully cut the initials *TQ* in the top crust and sprinkled lots of cinnamon and sugar on it. Three hours later, the men were drawn inside by the delicious smells coming from the warm kitchen. They were told to grab snacks from the trays full of finger food or a sandwich instead of sitting for a holiday meal just yet.

Anne gave the order, "Dinner will be served at one o'clock!"

TQ off-handedly remarked, "I can wait for the real thing. I've waited years already."

Fred and Paul looked at each other after TQ's revelation. This man didn't have a clue of what a family really was. He has missed out on so much.

Paul spoke so only Fred could hear, "Lots of mentoring, huh?"

Fred acknowledged with, "Yeah, but just think about it. We get to mold him the right way."

Both men were quiet as they considered the possibilities, and responsibilities which lie ahead.

Jim, overhearing, knew he had heard something important, but had no idea what it was about. Years later, he would observe the changes, remember, and understand.

Jim simply queried, "Is there a game on yet?"

Paul enthusiastically replied, "Pre-game, let's go." His actions were just as enthusiastic as he grabbed a whole tray of delicious snacks.

As the three men, snacks in hand, headed for the TV, TQ took two quick steps to reach Anne stirring a pot on the hot stove. He bent his head down over her shoulder and gently brushed the damp hair off her face to kiss her heat flushed cheek.

When Anne turned to look at him, TQ just smiled and said, "New tradition."

Anne smiled and repeated his previous remark, "I love traditions." They parted with the goofy smiles only those in love can so easily produce.

At precisely 1:00 P.M., the friends, old and new, held hands around the table as Paul asked the blessing on the food and each person there.

When Ann glanced at TQ, she saw his eyes glistening, close to tears. She realized what she took for granted must be a new and wonderfully moving experience to TQ. Her heart was committed to giving this man, her man, not just herself, but family, a real family. She would pray about that every day. She thought, *God, where is he? Does he know you?* Anne knew God had brought TQ into her life to be her husband. She also knew His word forbade unequal yoking. That must mean she was supposed to guide him, with a loving hand, to Jesus first. "Oh, help me Lord!" Anne prayerfully breathed the last to herself and God.

Paul sat directly across from "Katie," as he thought of her. She felt like "Katie" to him, exclusively for him. He was looking at her eyes when she caught his stare.

Katie blandly asked, "Do I have something on my face?"

Paul felt himself get as red as a twelve-year old schoolboy and had no answer.

Anne elbowed Katherine and grinned hugely. She grinned back at Anne with a knowing look which made Paul extremely uncomfortable. Katie thought dinner was a wonderful occasion!

Paul cleared his throat and asked, "Where are the pies I've been looking forward to all day? Anne, you did use your mom's recipe for the pumpkin pie, didn't you?"

Anne cheerily responded, "What else? We may have to wait on TQ and Jim. They may not be ready for desert for a couple of hours yet."

Jim leaned back in his chair and laughingly remarked, "Well, I'll just have to forego thirds and fourths for that pie."

TQ spoke around a mouthful of turkey, "I guess I'll just be skipping the fourths."

Katherine interjected, "I just love it when men appreciate great cooking."

Fred put his napkin on his plate and said, "Yes, this was great. In fact, it may have to be repeated next year."

Anne spoke directly to Katherine, "Katherine, you pour coffee, please, and I'll bring in the pies."

The ice cream and dessert plates were brought in and set before Paul. It would be his job to dish out the ice cream. As Katherine went back for coffee, Anne set the pies in the middle of the table.

TQ jumped up so quick his chair slammed into the wall behind him. They all looked at him, shocked to see his copper skin turn an ashen grey.

Fred found his voice and asked, "What's the matter boy?"

TQ asked, "Anne, where did you get that pie?" His voice betrayed a hint of frantic concern no one had seen in TQ before.

Anne answered, "I made it. You asked me to!"

TQ raised both hands, almost together to just under his chin and asked, "How did you know to make it like that? Do you have a recipe?"

Anne responded, "Yes! I got it yesterday from a nice man at the supermarket. He said you would like it."

TQ dropped back into the chair and forcefully directed Jim, "Jim, get your pad, your drawing stuff. Quick!"

Jim fairly launched himself into the other room for his "stuff."

Perplexed, Paul asked, "What is it? What's going on, TQ?"

Fred chimed in, "Yeah, what's got a hold of you?"

With an upraised hand, TQ said, "Wait! I have to be sure of something."

Katherine was standing in the doorway, holding the hot coffee and wondering what she had just missed.

TQ pointed to the coffee pot and said, "I think we'll all need that. Pour please!"

Katherine began to pour coffee around the stone silent table. Jim hastily settled his artist pad on the table where his plate had been but a moment ago.

Anne became white as TQ's description of Cypher came to life on the paper before Jim. She could see the nice young man in the supermarket. She could hear his voice tell her to put lots of cinnamon and sugar on top if it was for a man.

TQ waves his left hand toward the drawing and said, "Meet Cypher, everyone. He loves to bake. This is a specialty that he always made for me, with my initials in it. He knows I love that pie!"

Fred asks as he looks toward the windows, "Think we're made?"

Paul shook his head a couple of times and responded, "I doubt it. Wouldn't they have hit us by now if they knew where we were?"

16
Where, Where, Where?

TQ quickly remarked, "You're right! So, let's get a map and figure where they might be, before they do the same to us."

The table was quickly cleared and a local map was laid out.

Fred directed a question at Anne, "Anne, where's the highlighters? I think we'll need them."

Anne returned with a question of her own, "What highlighters?"

Jim, holding up a fist full of colored pencils, asks, "Colored pencils anyone? I have any flavor your like. There's cherry red, mint green, chocolate brown, and, of course, good old orange."

TQ waved a mint green pencil over the map and said, "Green for our location which is right about…"

Paul pointed, "Right here!"

Katherine looked at Ann and asked, "Where was that market, Anne?"

Anne placed her finger on the map, "Right there! It's right on the Northwest corner at the cross roads."

TQ asked the three people most familiar with the local area, "Where are the next closest markets to that one? We need all their locations. Mark them in blue."

Fred marked the locations and expresses, "Here is one and here are two more!"

Anne added, "This one's open all night." She pointed to another spot on the map about four miles south of the one where she met Cypher.

Fred adds another dot, "There is one more right over here. Why spot all the supermarkets?"

TQ's answer was for everyone's benefit, "Human nature! They went to the closest store to their safehouse. We can draw a line in red between points half way to each of the other stores from the one they shopped in. They are located within that area! Mark these points in red."

Paul admiringly concludes, "Now I know why you were the leader of that *Team*."

TQ responds with, "Each member is different than normal society, but only in minor ways. We all follow the larger patterns of living. Fred, connect those red dots with a red line."

Jim inquired, "What are we looking for? I'm new to the field and don't know which direction or what reasoning you all are using."

Fred replied, "Areas that are quiet, remote, wooded or hidden. They must have easy exits, but be hard to approach without being seen."

TQ, laughing, pokes Fred in the ribs, "You have that figured out pretty well for an old guy."

Fred hunched over and waved the red pencil like a cane. He replied, "Watch out or I'll beat you with my cane!"

Anne had a warm feeling at the friendly banter in a time of stress. She was blessed to have a father who trusted her instincts, and a man her father liked, too.

Jim suddenly exclaimed, "Hey guys, I know this area over here. I had an old maid aunt who lived on a dead-end road right here. I think the deed is still in the family, but not often used. People used to farm this area. There are several roads right here, here, and here. Old rutted dirt roads connect them through the woods about here. They are so old they aren't on the maps any more. I hunted there when I was a kid."

TQ smiled and encouraged Jim, "Go on! What else is there?"

Eyebrows knitted tightly, thinking back to long years ago, Jim replied, "There is or was a creek that runs through this area in the spring when the snow melts. It's a dry creek most of the year. Locals can take a four-wheel drive down it for fun. A tall bridge crosses the creek here. You can drive right under the bridge and get on the county road here. I think it's the old Borden place. They can be long gone before anybody is the wiser."

Pensively, Paul asked, "Any of these places have old barns with doors on both ends, like a wagon shed. They could hide vehicles in them. It would allow them to drive right out the back without being seen."

In response, Jim Fry said, "I haven't been there in fifteen years! If none of them have fallen down, I'd say there are seven or eight at most. One of them was on the Borden farm. There is a large pond the geese like just this side of that creek bridge." He marked the bridge location with an orange pencil. "The bridge is right about here. A dirt road goes all the way around that pond. I think I could get a couple of us close, unseen."

Leaning back in his chair, Fred flatly stated, "Too risky! If you are spotted with guns in the area, you'll scare them into moving. Or, worse, it could lead to civilian casualties."

Just as emphatically, Jim answered, "No, No, No! Cameras and my sketch pad are the keys. We are naturalists from some journal doing a wild life piece. We could even ask questions about the terrain and ways in and out. It would tell us what they know. It would be strictly fact-finding."

TQ acknowledged, "It might work!"

Anne raised her voice with a hint of a tremor, "You're not going, mister!"

Fred interjected with logic, "Of course he isn't. He's known. In fact, only Katherine and Jim are the unknown persons for sure."

Katherine quips, "I'm in! I'm tired of this apron already anyhow."

Pointing to himself, Paul asks, "Whoa! What about me?"

Katherine points at Jim, "If we were seen coming up here together in that rental, we already have a cover started and a connection to each other. We can't blow it now. It's our only sure cover and our greatest advantage."

TQ confirmed her point with, "She's right. Good thinking Katherine! Start in the morning."

Thinking of her evening dress and other clothes brought to impress Paul, Katherine informs them, "I don't have clothes for the woods and nature trails."

Anne gestures toward her bedroom and says, "Gotcha covered. Let them plan. We've got clothes to look at!"

The four men looked at each other and shook their heads as the two women headed for Anne's bedroom, already talking about what colors and styles would be nice for a hike in the woods at this time of year.

TQ, speaking to Jim, said, "You'll need credentials that will seem very real. I can't help or someone will blow the whistle on me to the *Team*. Money has no loyalties!"

Jim Fry replied, "Amen to that! BUT!" "He fairly shouted the last." "Do not despair my friends, because Mrs. Fry's little boy has some connections of his own. The credentials will be real. It may put us later in the morning than I'd like, but I know the editor of *American Wildlife* Magazine. He has been after me to draw this area for years. I'll tell him Katherine is a writer who wants to do a piece on waterfowl here and has asked me to do sketches. I'll offer him the piece and say we need credentials from the magazine to be allowed access to the land. He'll get them to us by fax or UPS in just a few hours."

Paul, with more than a hint of admiration in his voice, gave Jim new orders, "Great! Did you sign in at that motel on the way up like I told you to?" Jim nodded and Paul continued. "This is good so far. You two can't stay here now. Leave tonight and go to the motel. Call your friend from a cell phone immediately. Have him fax the letter of credentials to the motel. Each night just before dusk, go to the pier and talk to the old fisherman. We'll exchange info that way."

TQ looks around the table and asks, "Are you guys multi-tasking capable?"

Nods and murmurs of, 'Sure', 'Why?'

TQ, with a slight dipping of his head to the left side, the side where the pies were sitting on the counter, responds with, "Well, I know we have to get the other sketches done this afternoon, but I want to try that pie on for size!"

Fred hollered toward the bedroom, "Anne, hurry up! You've got a starving man out here! He hasn't eaten for a half hour!"

From the bedroom, Anne loudly exclaims, "Men, is that all they think about, their stomachs!"

Just as loudly Katherine replies, "There's another thing, but you aren't married yet."

Fred saw TQ's face light up red and Fred laughed to himself. He might live to see grandchildren yet!

The next three hours were spent by Jim and TQ constructing drawings of the rest of the *Team*. Jim's talent and TQ's memory brought the *Team* to life right on the kitchen table. The rest watched football games with half their minds on what the next few days would bring and occasionally giving due attention to pie a la mode.

17
Disintegration Starts

Toy looks in Spooky's direction and asks, "Spooky, you got those maps?" Spooky laid out the maps on the dining room table. "Good! What do we know that matters?"

Crimp quips, "TQ vanished like a ghost, again!"

Assertively, Toy, annoyance in her voice, said, "Stop the bull and pay attention! TQ DISAPPEARED! Somewhere, sometime he'll surface again. When he does, he'll be ready. We aren't the only bad asses out there. Did you ever think he might be putting together another *Team*? How would you like to face another *Team* he puts together? A *Team* you have no info on when he knows everything about us. That's why I brought in the extra people. He might not expect it. No more bull if you want to stay alive. He's a man. He needs food, shelter, clothing, weapons, and money. Money I'm sure he has cached all over the world or he wouldn't have attempted what he did." There were murmurs of assent.

Manny casually spoke, "I'm wondering about a few things,

1. If he is blowing the whistle, who to? We could ambush him there.
2. Where will he go for hardware?
3. How will he travel?"

Cypher returned with, "That's three more than I thought of."

Half-rising from his seat, Ricco replied, "I'm for action. I'm not good at planning this stuff."

BJ stood and addressed the group, "You guys are all missing it. It is overlooked more than anything else. Throughout history, the baddest dudes always had at least one woman. They were always their weakness. Who's his woman?"

Looking incredulous, Spooky returns, "He never seemed much attracted to women. He wasn't gay. He was just all business."

Rosalita walked among the *Team* and said, "I think BJ is right. How many of you haven't passed a couple holding hands or pushing a baby and longed for a little of that? It's natural!"

Crimp dryly answered, "But, there is no one! There never was any time for any of us to have that kind of a relationship."

Manny expressed the logic like it was so obvious it was hard for him to believe they all hadn't gotten the message before this. "Maybe that's the reason. Maybe that's why he wanted to pull out. The clock ticks on! We are all getting older. What do we have for all the time spent in dives, dusty deserts, swamps and jungles? Just suppose there is no other reason for his leaving than he just wanted more of a normal life, to be just another guy on the street."

Ruefully, Toy expressed, "If that's true, then we threw a rock at a wolf that just wanted to be left alone."

Ricco stood completely up and said, "Now we have to finish the job or get eaten by that wolf. When he gets to hunting, it is a terrible thing to watch. I don't want to watch him coming at me."

BJ, with a provocative look, asked, "Let's look at the whole picture. When he comes after us, I don't want to be unprepared. Where is he? We have to figure where he'd go if he just wanted to disappear. He's like an aborigine."

Spooky said, "What did you say?"

BJ said, "Aborigine."

Spooky, talking slightly down to BJ, replied, "Aborigines are in Australia. We have Indians here, remember. TQ is an Indian. He originally came from somewhere out West."

Crimp jumped in with, "Yeah, yeah, Arizona or Colorado I think!"

Rosalita concluded, "Maybe he is planning on going home. If he is wounded, and we know he is, he will go where he can get help from people that will not talk to a stranger or the law."

Conversationally, Peeper informed the group, "Arizona! He was raised by a grandfather on a Navajo reservation. Went on his own at fifteen after the old man died!"

Toy queried in an unbelieving tone, "How'd you know that?"

Peeper sneered, "I listen! You all talk. I think you're on the right track, though. We have to finish this one way or another, soon. Our lives are all at stake."

Toy explained, "We have to find out if he goes back to the reservation, back to family. We have to find that family."

Peeper waved his right hand over his head, "Piece of cake!"

BJ moved toward a bedroom and said over his shoulder, "Well, I'll be packing. Thanks for dinner!"

Bluntly Ricco asked, "Where you going?"

BJ stopped to explain, "You can't beat him there! You plan to go into a barren dessert looking for one aborigine, or Indian, that knows it like the back of his hand and can get hundreds of others to help him? Seen it and it's not pretty! If he is coming after me, he'll do it in my backyard! See ya, maybe! Good luck!"

BJ turned and went to retrieve his two bags. He called for a taxi from his cell phone as he retrieved two guns and a knife out of the smaller of his bags. He had stayed alive by not being a trusting man. He checked the loads in the weapons. All that talk had made him miss his family and the smell of his flower shop in California.

Toy waved her hand toward BJ's direction in dismissal, "Let him go. We know where he'll be if we want him. We have a much bigger fish to catch."

Crimp leaned forward and exclaimed, "Maybe that's it!"

Toy asked, with a hint of frustration, "What is 'IT'?"

Crimp said, "Fish, boats! He could be in any of a thousand boats tied up in these marinas or private docks on the lake."

With a discouraged voice, Cypher asked, "If he is, how do we find him?"

Spooky conjectured, "He won't be at an isolated, private dock – too easy to find him. The boat will be kind of plain, but fast, very fast."

Manny concluded, "It would have to be able to get him quite a distance, from here to, say, Canada. TQ could enlist a lot of help from other Indians up there. It's like a brotherhood between all those Indians when it comes to non-Indians."

Crimp tossed a question to the group, "What if he is still here? He was hurt."

Toy suddenly gave orders, "Ok, what we have to do is start looking in all the right places. Peeper! You and Cypher handle the Arizona angle; family, friends, home, and all that stuff. Manny, I see you got a weapon as soon as you arrived. You check on his purchases of hardware. Ricco! You and Spooky hold down the fort here. Rosalita! You, Crimp, and I are going shopping for boats. It's the best time of year. Owners will think we are hunting for a bargain. That'll be our excuse for looking at any boat still docked in the water."

Manny grabbed his jacket and said, "I'll get going now. Have to get the word out." He paused at the door and looked at Toy. "Holiday for two," was all he said.

Toy just sighed as she thought, with a new appreciation, of the man who just left.

Toy gave more orders. "We'll check the maps for marinas on a fifty-mile stretch. Split them in three sections and then hit the sack. Tomorrow is going to be a long day.

18
Unraveling

Dino, our street-wise valet, was puzzled. He was stuck in this flat while most of his contacts and expected answers were doing the *holiday thing*. Who ever heard of taking a holiday from selling information! Not only that, but what he had didn't fit together. Dino knew he could figure it out if he had the right pieces. What was worse, he knew others could, too. This was to be his ticket out of Chicago. He had no illusions. Dino may not get an offer to leave Chicago with Mr. Peck, even if he figured it out. It was a chance, probably his only chance at moving out of here, moving up in the world.

There was one piece of info that was interesting, but he couldn't make it fit anywhere. Two female cops were almost on top of the taxi explosion. They took the mystery man in the squad car to the clinic at the police academy. Dino verified, through a friend of the guard, the one named Donner stayed quite a while, left, then returned in civilian attire. She was there during the entire search for the guy.

The mystery man was why Mr. Peck was here. Dino was sure of it. What didn't compute was the guy disappearing from the compound, hurt, like he was a ghost or something. The only vehicle that left the place was the Donner lady. That was almost two hours after the search was started. Her old man was a big wig instructor there. She was a cop! That cleared her of suspicion, or did it?

The Donner chick couldn't be involved! Everything said she didn't know the guy. What if she did? Where would she take him if she did get him off the compound? His source at the precinct she worked out of said she took a couple weeks of vacation because she was upset about the explosion of the taxi. That was possible. However, from the accounts he could put together she didn't react that way at the scene of the taxi blast.

Dino had to find out two things:

Where is the girl?

Where is his man, Peck?

Dino glanced in the frying pan and expressed, "Crap! I burnt my hamburger!"

The ringtone on his cell started playing, *Who, who are you.*

Dino grabbed his cell phone. "Dino here! Mr. Peck, yeah, what can I do for you? 10:00 P.M., your place for brandy. How about a beer? I have some theories and some info you might be interested in. Sure, I can bring some clothes. Three days! I don't know. I've got others to… OH, OH, sure! I'll make it happen."

With no one else around, Dino talked to his hamburger. "A thousand a day! One large every day, plus expenses! I knew it! He's going to be my way out of here, to wherever. 8:45 P.M. now. I don't think he likes to wait! I got to get moving."

Pieces Come Together!

10:00 P.M., the door to room 1612 opened before Dino could knock. No one was standing in the door to greet him.

Mr. Peck's voice commanded quietly, "Come straight into the room. Set your bag and jacket on the couch, then, empty your pockets on the end table."

Dino replied, "Mr. Peck, I'm on your side!"

Manny countered with, "Then you won't mind doing what I said."

Dino shrugged and remarked, "Makes sense."

Dino complied with Manny's order.

In exasperation, Manny stated, "No weapons! You have no weapons!"

Dino responded, "Oh, I can use a pistol or automag pretty well, but most of my contacts get nervous around people that are packing."

Manny authoritatively demanded, "You get yourself a 40 automag or something else heavy that you can handle. Make it good, not fancy! You wanted to be in with me! Ok, but it might cost more than you are willing to pay. This is the only opportunity for you to walk. If you ever lie to me, you're dead. If you ever try to run when it gets hot, I'll kill you myself. I've never had a partner. I'm not sure I like it. Everyone out there knows I work alone."

With his hands raised to shoulder height Dino flatly announced, "I'm your ace in the hole!"

Manny, with enthusiasm, exclaimed, "That's great! Ace! You're Dino, out there, looking for information. Inside, you only answer to Ace! No one is to know you even have a first or last name. We'll talk about your theories and I'll give you lessons that might keep you alive, if you listen close! I'll only give them to you once. Time may be just that short!"

Ace asks, "When do we start?"

Manny explained in a softer tone, "We already have, kid. What's the info you have? Explain your theories to me!"

Ace gave Manny all the info he had jotted down on a note pad. As Manny read the notes, Ace explained how they fit into his loose theory of the Donner girl and her vehicle being the only way out of the clinic for the mystery man. The time, two hours after the hunt for the mystery man began, had Ace doubting his own theory. When he looked at his new partner, Manny was grinning so wide Ace thought his face would split.

Ace excitedly said, "I knew I had something. Let me in on what I had, have, or whatever?"

Smiling, Manny said, "You couldn't know without all the other info I have. You read these notes. Know them and then burn them and flush the ashes down the toilet. You'll get it long before you finish. I'll order pizza."

Ace offers, "Natoli's! 641-2800! Mention Dino and get free delivery."

Manny reaffirmed with, "Dino's not here! Ace asks no favors, gives none, and gets none. How's a supreme and some Heineken? I've a couple of other calls to make. You'll sleep in there, the second bedroom. Go in there, sit and read until food arrives. We may not get rest for quite awhile."

Ace headed to his new room and Manny made his calls. He ordered pizza and beer from Natoli's first. Manny dialed his second call.

BJ had just finished telling his wife and kids on the phone the flower show was boring and he would be home earlier than expected when his cell phone beeped in his ear. Call waiting! Who had this number? He quickly bid his wife good bye and connected to the waiting party.

BJ, in an explorative tone, said, "Yeah!"

Manny ignored BJ's obvious caution. "BJ, this is Manny Peck. Have you left yet?"

Still cautious, BJ drew out, "Noooooo."

Manny, with caution in his own voice, explained, "Something stinks in this. I've no love for TQ, but I have a bad feeling about the whole thing. After you left the room, a remark was made about knowing where you would be if they wanted you. I don't have a warm and fuzzy feeling about our new friends. I don't like being played!"

BJ replied, "Had the same feeling. It was my opportunity to walk and I took it. You didn't call to tell me how smart I am. What is it?"

Manny asked, "How does pizza and beer sound right about now?"

BJ remarked, "My family is expecting me home tomorrow."

Manny states, "We are a cold breed, but never turning on our own… not healthy. TQ is one of the smartest. He is also proven loyal.

We know what his old *Team* is about; except what they have planned for us when this is over."

BJ returned, positively, "You're right on for sure!"

Manny flatly stated his option, "You have thirty-five minutes to retrieve your weapons and get to my hotel before the pizza arrives. Here's the address…"

Ace ran out of the bedroom just as Manny hung up the cell phone. "I got it! I got it! We find the Donner girl and we find TQ! They'll be right where we would never think to look, right where they always hang out. Actually, it's probably where the Donner chick is."

Manny tucked the phone in his pocket and replied, "Right, Ace! Now, you get to find out where that place might be."

Ace looked Manny in the eye and said, "I don't ambush anybody, especially women."

Manny mused, "If it all goes as I think it will, no one gets hurt. Besides, the Ace in the hole stays hidden. You show only to protect my back."

Ace beamed, "That's me! We should get several new and clean cell phones. The untraceable throw-away phones will be best. Burn phones! Yours could be made."

Obviously pleased, Manny said, "Ahahh! I won't have to teach you as much as I thought. There is a guy coming here in twenty-eight minutes for pizza and beer. Take this earpiece and listen in from Natoli's. You get pizza and beer there. Remember, you don't exist. Find out where the girl would be. Get a weapon for you, and four new phones apiece. That's twelve phones. Call the room as Dino and ask if I want the Lexus serviced. Yes, means it's all clear and come up. No, come even faster. Have your new gun loaded and ready. Wait until tomorrow means come right at sunrise. Do it quiet!"

Ace waved toward the door, "Dino's going; Ace will return."

Manny handed Ace two thousand dollars. "Expenses!"

Manny opened the door and told Ace, "Go out the front. People need to see you leave here. This other man will probably use the stairs. Let the desk know you will be away visiting a sick aunt or something. Get that information as soon as you can and come up the stairs with the pizza."

At the Lake Cottage

Thanksgiving evening, 10:00 P.M., Special Agents Scott and Frey are heading out to the motel. As Special Agent Scott is entering the passenger door of the rental, she is stopped abruptly by someone grabbing her right hand in the dark. A strong grip held her hand firmly, then gently released it.

The now familiar voice of Paul Stanton whispered, "You better be very careful Katie Scott. I want you back here in one piece."

Katie softly replied, "I'm looking forward to returning to... this place."

Katie felt his hand gently squeeze her shoulder in a very familiar way that sent goose-bumps up her arms and neck. The door of the vehicle closed noiselessly and the garage door opened. Jim Frey eased them down the driveway and onto the road before turning on the lights of the car. Katie's mind was not on the one-sided conversation Jim maintained all the way to the motel. She kept hearing Paul's voice and the feel of his fingers on her shoulder.

19
A Light In The Darkness

At 1:00 A.M. TQ pulled on a dark blue wool jacket, and a black skull cap he found in the closet and stepped into the dark garage.

Paul's voice from the darkness abruptly stopped him, "Got the feeling, too, haven't you?"

TQ smiling into the darkened garage agrees, "Yeah! I don't know how much longer this place will be safe. Sooner or later someone will connect Anne with my disappearance. It scares me to death. I never had anything or anyone to care about before."

Paul, in a conciliatory tone, interjected, "I know. Fear for the safety of those you love can be almost over powering. It's the big one! It's the fear that can cripple you and make those very fears come true. Get beyond it. Be ready. Know the difference between your fear and your instincts. Use the fear to keep sharp, keep on the edge. Then, trust your training and instincts."

TQ quietly said, "I'm glad we're on the same side.

It was Paul's turn to grin into the darkness. "Me too, kid. You want the left or right?"

TQ expressed, "Right! Fifteen minutes we meet at the boat, cross over and work our way back here."

Paul opened the door and melted into the darkness to the left. TQ did the same to the right. Both were at the top of their awareness; nothing escaped their senses sharpened by a history of survival of the fittest. One learned in the jungles of Vietnam, the other in jungles of intrigue throughout the civilized world.

1:25 A.M., the small door on the side of the garage quietly opened to let Paul and TQ slip back in.

Fred admonished from the same darkness they left earlier, "About time you got back! How you expect a man to sleep with you two out in the night?"

TQ said, "Thought you were asleep!"

Fred raised an eyebrow no one could see and said dryly, "Yeah, right!"

Paul whispered, "Not so loud. We don't want to wake Anne."

Fred nodded toward the kitchen door as the three approached the same, "You can't wake her. She's sitting in the dark at the kitchen table with a fresh cup of coffee worrying about you two."

TQ had a quick feeling of pride and warmth in knowing Anne was waiting and worrying over him. Some day she wouldn't have to worry. He'd make sure of it.

As the three men entered the darkened kitchen together, TQ heard a soft sob come from the table. He took two long strides to the table and found her. Anne pressed her face into his neck. TQ felt the moistness of her tears on his skin and the tremble in her body.

He whispered, "We have a new tradition. The man always comes home to his woman."

Anne, after a pause and a sniff, whispered, "I love traditions."

Paul asked, "Where's the coffee?"

Fred looked at his daughter and TQ and said, "I think you better find it yourself. I'm going to bed."

Paul said, "If you two are going to be up keeping watch, or whatever, I'll sack out. Call me at four. You both need some rest, too."

TQ answered, "You're right! 4:00 A.M. it is. Anne, don't we have a tradition where the woman gets her man coffee when he comes home?"

Anne coyly remarked, "Not a tradition; it's my pleasure to take care of my man."

TQ held her tighter.

Anne explained the obvious to TQ. "First, my man has to let me go so I can get the coffee."

TQ whispered in her ear, "I think I want this more."

Anne sighed and said, "I know, but right now you need the coffee."

TQ complied, more than a bit reluctantly. Anne smiled at the thought.

As she picked up the pot and an empty cup, Anne asked, "Are you ready for this, for us, I mean?"

TQ pensively replied, "Three days ago I wouldn't have dreamed of this. Now, I find it hard to think of anything else."

Anne asked directly, "Do you know Jesus, God's son?"

TQ shrugged, "I know he exists is all."

Anne's face lit up as she explained, "It isn't the same. Even the Devil knows He exists! I'll help you learn about Him, know Him, trust Him. It's wonderful! He's wonderful! He gives me strength when I am weak. You got all your talents from Him."

TQ, in a doubtful voice, expressed, "Right! Like God wants me to be a killer!"

Anne explained, "No, not a killer, a soldier! The difference is God's will, right and wrong, good and evil. The difference is a relationship where God directs your life. You give up your will for His. Have you ever heard of King David?"

TQ answered, "I saw a famous statue of him, someplace."

Anne went on, "He is listed in the Bible as one of the faithful. God said he was a man after God's own heart. He also was the most efficient soldier ever in hand-to-hand combat. The women sang that King Saul killed his thousands, but David killed his tens of thousands. You be a soldier, if that is what God wants. I will be your wife when you find

God through Jesus, and find out what God wants you to be. When you find out what that is, let him direct your life."

In exasperation, TQ said, "I don't know how!"

Anne offered, "I'll help."

She handed him the coffee. They stood close in the dark, sipping coffee and thinking of how it all came to be. Anne was thinking of how the Master makes his plans and what others mean for harm comes to good for those who love God. TQ was wondering how it could all come about. He was realizing he was not in control, but not sure he was ready to relinquish that control. It felt good in a way, but it also left him feeling a little anxious. He had been on his own, making decisions, since he was fifteen. TQ didn't know how to let anyone, even God, make decisions for his life. He didn't trust anyone, not even God, at this point.

20
The False Path

Toy was restless. Her mind was racing! How did this all start? Why didn't they just let TQ go? He would never turn them in. Envy and jealousy! TQ could just make up his mind to change and live like the rest of the world. The *Team* was trapped in circumstance by their own individual weaknesses and fears. They were a *Team* of unparalleled assassins afraid to make a change for the good. Was it too late? As little as a week ago, Toy would have slammed anyone who suggested anything but this life she lived. Watching the *Team* fall apart as individuals and a unit had her perplexed and unsure. It started her wondering what else there was for the *Team*. What else was possible for her, Toy? Manny! She knew he was playing her game. Toy knew Manny was better at it. Maybe she could change his mind if she had enough time, if she was honest with him. Something about Manny was honest and demanded she be honest.

BJ leaving was like a signal. No one said anything, but she saw the shadows of uncertainty crawl over all their faces. She felt fear enter her own heart. Manny knew what to do. He was a lot like TQ. Toy just wasn't sure if what Manny planned to do was what the *Team* wanted to do. She didn't know what to do to stop him. Toy wasn't sure she would or could stop him if she knew his plan. Was she already leaving the *Team*?

Toy thought to herself, *why am I so confused? 4:00 A.M., but I can't rest. I might as well get up! I'll get a hot bath before the others get up. It's going to be a long day.*

6:45 A.M. – breakfast had been unusually quiet. BJ's leaving abruptly yesterday had caught them all off guard. The realization he had done the very thing TQ had attempted made each of them evaluate their motives and actions, all except Ricco, that is. Before breakfast, he had lay awake wondering why Toy hadn't told him to whack BJ. He didn't like BJ, anyway. He would like to off Manny with the better-than-you attitude, too. Maybe Toy wasn't the right one to lead the *Team*! Action, where's the action?

During breakfast, each person there had memories of past regrets, discouragement, and uncertainty about the future. No one voiced their thoughts to the others.

The phone rang and Cypher actually jumped.

Crimp grabbed the phone and tossed it to Spooky. The move was not lost on Toy. Spooky answered the phone. "Harris! Spooky, yeah! Where you at, Callahan? Rosalita is here and Manny is just pulling in. We decided we didn't need BJ's services. He went home. No, Manny stays in the city. We all have jobs to do. Toy's in charge. You need to talk to her."

Spooky tossed the phone to Toy at the other end of the table.

Toy deftly caught the phone. She spoke directly into the mic, "Long time no see, Bruce. Sure! Peeper will meet you at the truck stop. Yeah, that's the one. Don't go in. Park in the back of the restaurant area and wait. He'll be there in about forty minutes to an hour. What kind of vehicle did you get? No kidding! See you after lunch. We are going out to look for TQ. Yessss, the Ghost vanished again! Thanks for reminding me." She exclaimed as she hung up the phone, "Jerk! What are we waiting for? He's not going to just walk in here and say shoot me. Peeper, you get Callahan at the truck stop."

21
Recon Begins

At the Motel

By 6:00 A.M., Katherine Scott was up and ready for breakfast. She was debating whether she should watch the local news channel for an hour before knocking on Jim's door when the ring of her telephone gave her a start.

Katherine spoke into the cell phone, "Katherine Scott here. Jim! No, you didn't wake me. I was waiting 'til 7:00 before I knocked on your door. 5:00am, always! I didn't think artists got up that early! Sure, I'm ready for breakfast. I'll get my coat and meet you at the car."

In the car headed for the truck stop and breakfast, Jim explained, "I think we should look at the local map. We can figure the perimeter roads around the area that we are to check out. We have all day to do it. We'll make notes on what we find and pass it to Paul this afternoon. We should pick up some trail mix, etc. so we look like naturalists in case we are spotted and confronted on a back road.

Katherine asks, "How about an hour or so at a library or book store. We can gain knowledge on the local waterfowl that way."

Jim replied, "As soon as they open. Truck stops have a lot of books, too. We'll look through what they have. We can buy a local map there and ask about the ponds and lakes in the area. It will give us more credibility."

Katherine complimented Jim, "Hey, I think you should put in for field duty. You're right on!"

Jim returned with, "I thought about it once. I decided instead to put the talents God gave me to their best use. I'm an artist. Some say I'm pretty good. I have my own studio at home. However, most artists starve. I like to eat! So, I took the job at the FBI. What I do for the FBI is not art."

Katherine made a request, "Bring some of your art into the office. I'd love to see them."

Jim announced, "Time to become naturalists. We're here!"

Katherine was amazed at how Jim Frey's personality and natural gift of gab had locals and truckers standing three deep around their table. They were all trying to point out the best places to find types of waterfowl Katherine had no idea ever existed. Jim dutifully made marks on the map and created a neat legend on the side of the map which seemed to greatly impress the thirty plus hearty men in baseball caps and Carhart jackets. After breakfast and two cups of coffee, she politely excused herself and headed toward the Ladies room at the rear of the restaurant portion of the truck stop.

She glanced out the back door of the diner and froze in her tracks. That guy standing outside the bronze Hummer II and talking to the driver! Get the license number. No pen, no paper! Just then, a trucker came out of the men's room.

Katherine tapped the trucker's arm and asked, "Excuse me. Do you have a pen or pencil I could borrow?"

The trucker pulled a pen from his pocket, "Keep it."

Katherine waved the pen, "Thank you so much!"

Katherine wrote on the palm of her hand, IL- 48G26, bronze Hummer II, white male, 28-33 years old, funny shaped hat. Other male, outside the vehicle, black, medium brown complexion, about 5'6", well-built, short hair, getting into a late model blue SUV. Which way are they going? East, toward our friends!

She hurried back to the table, completely forgetting why she went to the back of the diner.

Katherine politely interrupted, "Jim, I hate to cut this short, but I just got a message. We must get in touch with the boss immediately. Will you gentlemen excuse us? Thank you so much for the tips and information. You are all so kind."

Jim didn't miss a beat. He rolled the map and scooped up his pencils. He thanked the ball caps as he hurried after Katherine. He could tell she was struggling to contain her excitement as they stowed the equipment in the back seat and buckled themselves in the front.

Katherine directed Jim. "Go East, legal, but quick."

Jim said, "Spill it!"

Katherine asked, "Where's your sketch bag?"

Jim answered, "At the motel, I didn't want to get caught with it."

Katherine excitedly said, "I saw one. He was talking to someone in a bronze Hummer II. They left going East, in two vehicles. I wrote it all on my hand. I'll put it on this pad. There, done! Map, where's the map?" Katherine jabbed the map with her finger. Here, we are right here! Where did you say those old barns were, Jim?"

Jim replied, "Two streets up on the right is the first one. I don't like going in blind like this. Maybe we should have back-up. We better call Paul Stanton. Use the cell number he gave us."

Katherine punched in 'Memory, 2' on the cell and listened as it rang. On the fourth ring she heard, "Hi, it's Fred."

Katherine asked, "Where's Paul? I have info on our close relatives. Two cousins have arrived."

Fred exclaimed, "Great news! Do you know where they'll stay tonight? Paul would be delighted to go see them."

Katherine explained, "Not yet, but we're hopefully following them home. We lost them for the time being."

Fred said, "Ok, send our best."

Katherine answered, "Later, when the whole family can surprise them!"

Fred concurred with, "Great idea. Keep in touch and definitely let us know where you are."

Katherine responded with, "Sure thing! Say 'Hi' to Paul and the others."

She opened the glove box and pushed a small orange button which activated the portable tracking device the Bureau installed before they started this. It would be removed before the rental was returned.

Katherine wistfully said, "Jim, I hope this thing works."

Jim confided, "I checked it before we left this morning. We're good. Let's start looking down these roads. Get out the camera and look like a naturalist."

Back at the Cottage

TQ wasn't in the cottage. Fred and Paul had checked the garage, grounds, and the boat. The weather had changed in a hurry. This fall had been mild compared to previous years. The Canadian cold was dropping into the U. S. and bringing snow, eight to twelve inches of snow was due to arrive and it was well on its way. There goes the boat! No one will be able to be on the water with the cold building ice on the lake and the waves bouncing the boats around like toys in a bathtub.

Anne was unconcerned. In fact, she was humming.

Fred demanded, "Ok, where did he go?"

Anne smiled and said, "Don't know. He didn't say. He thought I was asleep."

Fred asked, "What's that?"

Paul repeated her words, "He thought you were asleep?"

Anne, smiling, said, "Uuh huh! It's a tradition. You started it, Dad."

Fred demanded, "Me! Speak English, girl!"

Paul, in a voice of consternation said, "Yes, please, I'm lost."

Anne explained this way, "Dad, you never left the house without kissing mom. She told me it was tradition. I told TQ. We didn't go to bed until after his watch. He came in my room a half hour later like… well, like a Ghost. There was no noise at all when he walked. No creaking floor or anything. He kissed me on the cheek and whispered, 'I love traditions.' Before I could call to him he was gone – vanished. That's how I know he'll be back."

Fred wagged his head and said, "There's no logic there at all."

Paul smiled at Anne and told Fred, "You're correct, but I won't bet against it. I'll pour coffee. It's nasty out there."

As Paul was pouring the third cup of coffee, TQ spoke directly behind him. Paul yelped as he jerked and spilled hot coffee on his hand.

Paul yelled, "Owwww! Where'd you come from and where have you been? Don't you need sleep?"

Before he answered, TQ crossed to Anne who turned her cheek to receive the peck TQ placed there.

TQ shrugged his thick shoulders and stated, "Why, I had to think. There's nothing like a good recon to clear the mind and come up with answers. I woke up thinking that we had no planned escape routes or meeting places."

Paul mused, "If they came in this weather, we could sneak out easy."

TQ explained, "Not so! We don't know how many there are or what way they would come in. That leaves us at a disadvantage. This garage has a side door. The side door on the neighbor's garage faces this one. It's only twenty-two feet between the doors. A quick dash and some or all could be in that garage. You could lock the door from the inside and hide on the floor boards of the old caddy in there. I took the liberty of unlocking the door to the garage and the caddy. I also disconnected the fuse so the lights wouldn't come on when the doors of the caddy are opened. There are also three ways through the housing area on this side of the road. There are two more through the marina side. There aren't but two ways to exit the area during the day without being seen. We must go to a lot of the cabins and walk around to make it harder for anyone to tell just what cabin we would be in."

Anne asked, "So, what do we do?"

Fred added this information, "This is a community. There is a community house that has a safe where we store a back-door key for every cottage in the place. I happen to be on the board. We don't have to break in anywhere. And, most people are gone for the winter. I'll get the keys. You and Paul can check them out during the bad weather."

Paul said, "Sounds like a plan. We'll leave right after the French toast and sausage Anne's making."

TQ added, "Yep, sounds like a plan. I'll set the table."

Fred exclaimed, "Well Anne, he was easy to train!"

Anne looked at the two older men and said, "You two could take lessons from TQ."

Grinning, TQ expressed, "You know what they say about old dogs."

Paul, with mock affront, exclaimed, "Hey, what did I do? Leave me out of this."

Fred looked at Paul and said, "Traitor!"

Fred filled them in on the phone call from Katherine. The table was set and grace said in less than three minutes. Plans for the day were made between bites of breakfast and sips of hot coffee.

22
Found Out

Peeper pulled up to the old barn, jumped out, and swung open the double doors. He motioned Callahan to pull the Hummer in. Then, he pulled the SUV in and closed the doors. They had almost reached the door to the house when an SUV stopped out front.

A lady opened her window, hollered, and waved. Callahan hung back as Peeper slowly approached the vehicle.

Peeper asked in short tones, "What do you want?"

Katherine gave this explanation, "We're from *American Wildlife* Magazine! The nice people at the truck stop said a great place to observe the migrating waterfowl was Reed's Pond. Are we close?"

Peeper wagged his head and replied, "Sorry, we aren't local either. Try a couple of places down that way. The old folks there could probably help you."

Katherine apologetically answered, "You look like the outdoors type, hunters. I thought maybe you would know. Sorry!"

Peeper said, "Sure, you just got the wrong guys."

Katherine waved, "Well, have a good day. Bye!"

Peeper half raised a hand, "Bye!"

As peeper joined Callahan, he said, "She was a looker!"

Callahan frowned and said, "She looks like trouble. All good-looking women are bloody trouble. Observe ducks and stuff! They are bloody crazy to go out in this weather, if you ask me!"

As they entered the house, Peeper hollered out, "Bruce is here. You should see that Hummer he's driving. It's all powered up!"

Cypher hollered from another room, "Yo! Peeper, you were the one listening. Do you have a clue about the name of that reservation? There are a number in each of those western states. The computer is full of them."

Peeper hollered back, "Try Arizona, close to Phoenix, I think. Stick to the reservations for the Navajo."

Bruce looked at Peeper and asked, "What, mate? Is this TQ a bloody aborigine?"

Peeper replied, "You're the second one to call him that!"

Bruce observed, "Don't know much about the bloke. Why do you need me? I been thinking; you guys can all drive well enough for this job."

Cypher explained, "We don't want your skills to get us in. We need you around to get us out. You have border contacts and know Canada. We all have new passports and papers. Everyone wants to live long enough to use them."

Bruce informed the group of what the word on the street was, "The word is coming out that a number of 'Agencies' are not happy about all this. You guys might be out in the cold if it isn't over in the next forty-eight hours."

Spooky ignored the comment, pointed to the old barn, and directed Bruce, "Go see Ricco! He is outside checking the lay of the land. He'll show you all the important terrain features and you will be briefed when you get back in."

Spooky continued, "There are a few things bugging me. Take that young lady cop. She goes back to that clinic after her tour of duty. She's there when TQ vanishes. Then, she disappears, too. I think Rosalita and BJ were on to something. We need to check out that angle."

Manny spoke up while stomping snow off his boots as he came in from the snowy cold. "You are sooooo right, Spooky! So, what's your take on it?"

Spooky emphatically stated, "Trouble! No doubt about it."

Manny asked, "Where are Toy and the others?"

Spooky gave part of the answer, "Ricco's outside checking exits and terrain… needed action."

Peeper filled in the rest with, "The other three are checking all the marinas for fifty miles along the lake."

Manny confirmed their actions. "They're on the right track. The way I have it figured, from my sources, is there are three of them that we can be sure of. If we are sure of three, there must be more. I don't like unknowns. They're deadly!"

Ricco slapped snow from his clothes as he stepped in and stated, "We're the best! We can handle any twenty other personnel. I'll say it for all of us. TQ scares the hell out of all of us; those of us that know him well, that is!"

Crimp told Ricco, "Manny has a lead!"

Ricco excitedly said, "That's what I'm waiting for! How soon do we move in?"

Spooky, a little tersely, answered, "Not until Toy says so."

Ricco impatiently stated, "Hey, if we can end this now, I say we get it on!"

Manny looked directly at Ricco and said, "You know Ricco, I just figured out why we aren't friends."

Ricco looked back and growled, "Yeah, why?"

Manny's voice took on the tone of a father explaining why his son should wear shoes while walking on broken glass, "Being close to stupid people can get you killed. You're dumber than a box of rocks!"

Enraged, Ricco's knife flashed into his hand as if by magic and flew through the air to land harmlessly by the stove as Manny's foot completed its arch after contacting Ricco's hand.

Spooky jumped between them with a hand toward each of the two men.

Spooky raised his voice, "Hey, if we're at each other, we are already dead men! Knock this crap off! Ricco, you need to take some lessons from Cypher here. Listen more before you act. You'll live longer! I watched Manny in action in Kenya. Manny, you baited him. Stop it right now!"

Manny shrugged and expressed, "Sure, you're right. I just don't like loose cannons. He jumps the gun before he has all the Intel."

Ricco looked around at the others and said, "I want to live, too. This waiting gives me fits."

Manny held up the palm of his hand and stated, "Just a little while longer. We'll go over my Intel when Toy and the others get back."

Ricco, smiling, said, "Sorry! I'll take it as good news. It'll be worth the wait." To himself, he thought, *Then I'll off you Manny, and I'll really enjoy it.*

Manny was looking at the eyes behind the smile. He wasn't fooled a bit. He was glad he had an 'Ace in the hole.'

23
Plans

By 10:30 A.M., Fred and Paul had finalized several portions of a plan, one part at a time.

TQ had been monitoring the tracking signal from Jim and Katherine's vehicle by highlighting their movements and putting orange dots on the map where they stopped.

TQ caught their attention with, "Guys, their vehicle went down this road and stopped right near the end. Then, they drove to each of the next two streets, but only went in a hundred feet or so. They paused at each then moved on and crossed to the county road here. Now they are stopped by that bridge over the dry creek bed. It isn't too far from the first place they stopped. I think they found something!"

Paul worriedly stated, "TQ, Anne, we aren't waiting any longer to relocate the two of you. We can't go through official channels or we risk a leak."

Fred broke in, "That idea I was thinking about, well, here it is! I'll have Doc Bailey get an ambulance with sirens, lights, the works, to come next door. We'll move Anne out on a stretcher. The three of us will exchange clothes with Doc and two cops. We all go out in the ambulance. The ambulance rolls out with one local cop car in front. A second hangs around until they are sure it's clear. Then, Doc and the two others climb in with the driver and off they go to the precinct. We leave lights on over here and the TV playing a movie. If it's clear, Paul and I can come back here and close this place up. You two will be long gone to wherever TQ knows is safe."

Emotionally, Anne expressed, "No Dad! We have to go together. You must come, too."

Paul explained, "It would be a dead giveaway. The more who try to travel together, the easier they are to find."

TQ held both of Anne's hands and said, "They're right, Anne. It's not just me or you, it's us. They are unselfishly giving all they have for us. You and I, we're their future! It might only be a short while. I think most of them will give it up after a few months. Well, half of them, anyway. I know them. Ricco will stay on the trail, but he needs a leader. Crimp and Cypher are thinkers. They'll lose interest in us and leave. The *Team* will start to break up. Peeper will stick with Ricco because he has no other life. He won't fit in anywhere, even though he can physically blend in very well. He's an emotional outcast."

Anne asked the important question, "What about Spooky and Toy?"

TQ took a deep breath and answered, "Therein lies the problem! If they would quit chasing me, they could do what they do best, be operatives for Uncle Sam. If only Toy leads, I'm sure it would fail. She's good. Toy just doesn't know how good she is. She would be self-defeating. Spooky has intuition. It's uncanny for certain. However, he lacks the planning and drive necessary to lead. He has no focus. If either one stays with the team, we'll have to hide really well for at least a year. If they learn to work together, as leaders, we'll be in big trouble. We'll need new identities. We can't use the US Marshal's office. Toy has friends there, and in the FBI. Spooky has the CIA covered. What about your connections, Paul?"

Paul explained, "We aren't allowed to hide anything from those agencies. You realize you'll need at least three identities and papers to back them up."

The lights of a car flashed in the driveway.

Fred motioned Paul and TQ back and said, "You two stay in the kitchen. Anne, you follow me with a gun under your apron. We'll see who it is. Paul, watch the back while we are at the front door. TQ, stay out of sight."

Fred opened the front door to the second knock. In the doorway was a Domino's pizza delivery man. He had the car, shirt, hat and hot-box in hand. The name tag on his shirt said, '*Bernie*'.

Bernie looked at Fred, then Anne, then back to Fred and said, "Excuse me. I think some kids must have pulled a fast one on us again. A Sammy ordered three supreme pizzas for a party at this address. Don't suppose you're throwing a party?"

Fred smiled and replied to Bernie, "You've been had Bernie. Tell you what I'll do; I'll take two of those off your hands. What's the price for two?"

Bernie looked at the hotbox in his hand and said, "Well, it was thirty-five dollars with delivery for all three. You give me twenty-five and you get to keep all three."

Fred retorts, "How about twenty dollars?"

In exasperation, Anne said, "Dad, give him the twenty-five. He came all the way out here in the snow for a prank."

Fred resignedly said, "Honey, you got a lot to learn. It isn't the pizza or the money. It's the bartering that's the fun."

Bernie raised one eyebrow in Anne's direction and said, "Afraid he's got you there, but I'll take the twenty-five you offered!"

Anne handed him the money, "Here, it's a very silly game you men play."

Fred looked at Bernie, "Women!"

Bernie replied, "Hey, I've got no clue either!"

Fred and Anne carried the pizza to the kitchen as Bernie turned the corner. Bernie turned off the car lights and pulled in behind a cottage. He could look straight through the windows of the empty garage and observe the cottage he just left. After ten minutes, he pulled out the silver cell phone and punched the speed dial.

24
Paths Defined

In less than two hours, Toy, Rose, and Crimp returned from the marinas. There were very few people available to talk to. All but a few cottages were closed up for the winter and the weather was getting bad. As soon as they entered the door, Ricco told them Manny had some important information.

When Toy asked him what it was, Manny gave Toy a smile that warmed her heart and said, "Good things are worth waiting for."

A cell phone rang in Manny's pocket to the tune of Dixie. It rang a second time, a third time, and a fourth time before it stopped.

Spooky looked to Manny's coat pocket and up at Manny's face before he said, "What's the matter? Is that some old girlfriend you don't want to talk to?"

Manny simply got two glasses and poured some of his special brandy into them. He handed one to Ricco, tapped his glass, and said, "Time for action!"

Ricco went blank for a second, then smiled and said, "Bravo my friend!"

Manny dryly replied, "I'm still not your friend."

Toy demanded, "Well, what is it?"

Manny swirled the brandy and said, "There are four of them in a cottage about four miles from here."

He swirled his brandy again, sipped, and answered their masked question, "Just because I usually work alone doesn't mean I haven't any friends, contacts, or backup."

Here he pointedly sent his gaze around the room and looked each person directly in the eye. He finished with Toy. Toy turned ashen, then, pink in the cheeks.

Manny thought, "Not so cold after all!"

Spooky stepped in the center of the group and said, "Hey, we're in this together. We have to trust each other."

Manny pointedly answered, "We're in it, yes. Trust? Not in this life time! What's your gut tell you, Spooky? Mine says some people are going to die. It's not going to be just those four in the cottage. It's not going to be me! Tomorrow's another day."

Ricco demanded, "Where is he? Which cottage?"

Manny looked at Spooky and nodded toward Ricco, "Loose cannon! The snow is supposed to be worse tomorrow. See you about 6:00 A.M. Hopefully we'll be gone our separate ways by 8:30 A.M." He paused at the door and looked at Toy. "I thought there might be more. I really hoped so!"

Toy moved toward where her coat hung, "I'll see you to your car. The rest of you look to your weapons, vehicles, passports, and papers. We travel light. Wipe this place clean after tomorrow's breakfast. That will be 6:00 A.M."

As she reached for her jacket, Manny fluidly intercepted her and held the coat out for her to put on. She dutifully turned and slipped into her coat as if it happened every day. He then held the door for her to pass through. Toy walked with him to the Lexus.

Manny held the passenger door open for her to get in. Toy looked at Manny's face and seated herself in the passenger seat without a word. Manny got in behind the steering wheel.

In the car, Manny turned to Toy and said, "We can speak now. The first issue is TQ. I don't want it between us. I came here and spotted your vulnerability, what you really want out of life. Don't look surprised! I'm gifted there. What I didn't count on was the way I'd grow to feel about you. I don't want a holiday for two. I won't accept it! I want lots of holidays! If TQ wants out for a woman, I totally understand! We both understand commitment or we wouldn't be here, now. I won't be here tomorrow. I'm out! All my information says you guys panicked. I'll give you the Intel on where to find them at 6:00 A.M. by phone, if you still want it. Can you quit now?"

In a hoarse whisper Toy answered, "I want to."

Manny stated, "But, you can't."

Toy sorrowfully expressed, "I'm their leader, elected by my peers."

Manny snorted and pointed toward the house. "They're not your peers. You're better, much better! Good things, the things you covertly fight to protect, you should have. We can have them, you and me!"

Toy, with tears, real tears, streaming down her cheeks, choked out, "I don't know what to do!"

Manny softened his voice and said, "Lead them! If you live, go to the Manchester Hotel in Boston, room 1104. A man named Ace will know it. He will bring pizza to you. Read the message on the inside of the lid."

Toy resignedly said, "I want to go now, but I can't. I must see it through."

Manny took her hand in his and said, "I know. I wanted the first, but knew I would only be able to trust you to stick with me if you were true to your word. I'll wait in Boston for the outcome."

Toy was crying, sobbing now. Manny tilted up her chin. He kissed her forehead, her nose, then, her lips. He removed a clean handkerchief from his suit jacket and wiped tears from her eyes and cheeks.

Manny gave her this directive, "If it goes bad, don't trust any of them. Run to Boston!"

Toy, thinking of the recent events, said, "Funny how TQ turned from this life, BJ left, and now you. I want to be out of it, too. TQ had the right idea. We just couldn't see it."

Toy handed him back the handkerchief and, with a sorrowful look, closed the car door behind her and walked, head down, into the house. Manny watched until the door closed behind her.

25
Revelation

The shadows on the curtained windows of the cottage told Ace there were four people in the house. At the precise time, he called Manny Peck and let the phone ring four times before hanging up. He returned the clothes and car to his cousin, Bernie, along with the promised two hundred dollars and the twenty-five from the lady at the cottage as a tip. He had already paid Bernie for the pizzas in advance. Then, he was off to the hotel to meet Mr. Peck. Manny wasn't that much older than Ace, but Ace couldn't help calling him Mr. Peck. He had never had much respect for authority in general. Mr. Peck was different. He was straight, and he didn't do drugs. Mr. Peck hardly even drank. He just sipped a little brandy once in a while.

On the way back to his hotel room, Manny pondered the way life turned on the small things. Toy had said he was turning away from this life of danger, intrigue and secrecy. The cloak and dagger life had made him seem special. The faces in the night made him know it was wrong. There were those times late at night when he would pick up a Gideon and read until he could sleep. Nothing else helped him to sleep. Nothing else gave peace. Most of it he couldn't understand.

Manny thought, "Why not, I'm smarter than most." What was that one passage he read? It said he would not be able to understand the Bible until he made Jesus the Lord of his life. Come on, the guy's dead! They killed him! Or, had they?

Yeah, Manny wanted out. He had to meet TQ face to face first. That would tell him everything, verify his conclusions.

Back in the hotel room, the green cell phone rang twice and stopped. Manny wiped down his weapon and checked the loads in the eight, fifteen round magazines. He handled one of the frags, put it in his pocket, then, took it out of his pocket and tossed it on the couch by the other one.

The green cell phone rang again. He picked it up and hit the talk button. "Ten minutes", was all he said. Manny dialed Ace and repeated, "Ten minutes."

At the Cottage

Anne had been reading TQ passages from Romans, Ephesians, John, Matthew, Isaiah, and Proverbs for the last three hours. TQ had questions, so many questions. Sometimes her Dad or Paul would help where she wasn't sure of the answers.

TQ asked, "How come I never knew this before? Why don't you tell people? So many people don't know about Jesus!"

Fred answered, "That's called missions or evangelism. Jesus said to take the gospel into all of the world! There are individuals and organizations doing just that. The problem is every new generation has to be told. We never seem to get caught up with the population growth."

TQ shook his head slightly and said, "This is a lot. I'm going to go to bed early so I can think on it."

Paul asked, "Recon?"

TQ nodded and said, "I'm getting a bad feeling. Let's do it at 2:30 A.M. and again at 4:00 A.M."

Fred informed the other three, "The stage is set for my call to Doc Bailey, any time from 5:00AM to 9:00AM. They are standing by not more than three miles from here."

Anne spoke to TQ, "TQ, walk with me through the marina. I'll miss this place if I never come back. I know it's risky. Please!"

Fred's voice showed his exasperation as he said, "Girl, you're putting TQ in a tough spot, and both of you at risk."

Anne's voice begged understanding, "Dad, I need to see it once more. I want to walk where mom walked with me when I was a little girl. I want to absorb it so I can tell my children."

Paul said to TQ, "Put on those old fisherman boots. We'll get you a grey wig and a skull cap. Walk with a slight shuffle or limp and use this cane. Bend slightly at the shoulders to look older. I'll be flanking you on the left all the way. That ok with you Fred?"

Before Fred could answer, TQ said to Anne, "Hopefully it won't be the last time, but it will be quite awhile I'm sure."

Paul left the garage precisely 90 seconds before Anne held the arm of the old fisherman, steadying his walk toward the marina and old memories. At the same time, they were quietly making new memories.

Paul watched the other shadows as he moved along the flank of the young couple. He had that once! He let the job get in the way, between him and his first wife. He rationalized, then, he was doing it for her, for family. Really, it was pride. He was proud to be in his job. He liked the feeling of esteem he got from it. He lost, lost big! Pride cost him so much! Could he do it again? Had God given him a second chance with Katie? He hardly knew her. What, it had only been less than a week!

Paul whispered a prayer as he watched TQ and Anne, "Lord, look after them. Protect them and give them a long life of love for you and each other."

The snow fell like brilliant white diamonds in the street lights as the couple crossed the street. The silence continued like a blanket of peace wrapped snugly about the shuffling old man and pretty young woman, arm in arm, winding their way among the boats of the marina.

TQ didn't know how to say what he felt. He was a leader of men. It came easy. To talk to a woman of what was in his heart was beyond him right now. He had no clue what to do. Anne seemed content to just hold his arm and lean on him. TQ loved the poetry in nature. He loved how the good, the bad, the beautiful, and the ugly all were woven together like a painting of life by a master hand.

In his mind, TQ concluded, "The very form and function of nature proves that God exists! If something new evolved, it would throw the balance of nature off. It seems so logical. If God is real, nature is real, people are real. People are sinners; I'm a sinner! Heaven is real. Hell is real. Jesus is real! He was sent to save me. God must love me! I don't deserve it, but I sure will take it. I don't know why you love me, God, but thanks. Thank you for Anne, too. I promise to take care of her if you will show me how."

TQ whispered loudly, "Anne, I know! I mean, I really know!"

Anne asked, "Know what?"

TQ, louder this time, "God! God is real! Jesus is real! The whole Bible is true. I found it hard to believe that God will forgive me for all I've done, but I accept that forgiveness. I'm going to do what he wants from now on."

Anne said not a word out loud. She held tighter to TQ's arm as tears of joy flowed off her chin and a prayer of thanks went to God.

This newly made memory was sufficient for both. They turned and went directly back to the cottage. Paul came in the back almost as they entered the front of the cottage.

Fred stopped his pacing and let out an audible sigh. He had been worried though he knew he shouldn't have. He had put them in the care of his two best friends, Jesus and Paul.

In a voice of consternation, Paul stated, "Boy, what's the matter with you? You dropped the disguise and fairly flew back here. What's wrong?"

Anne joyfully interjected, "Not a thing. I can get married!"

Dumbfounded Fred asked, "Anne, what are you talking about?"

Anne fairly shouted, "Unequally yoked! Prayer, answered prayer! Let TQ tell you."

TQ waved both hands and exploded, "Jesus is real!"

Paul answered with slight frustration, "Certainly! I know that."

TQ responded in a husky voice, "I didn't. He is real. He loves me. And, now I love him. He's not a ghost. He's real!"

Fred voiced it this way, "Thank you God!"

TQ excitedly asked, "What else do I have to do? There must be more, something else."

Anne counted off on her fingers, "Let's see. Repent—done! Be baptized! We'll have to wait for warmer weather or a larger tub! Confess Jesus to others, tell someone!"

Paul held up a hand and explained, "God knows. He'll work things out. Start out right now with faith, stand on it."

TQ took a deep breath and expressed, "I feel great. It feels like I just woke up from a long-needed rest in the cool damp forest."

Fred nodded and said, "Peaceful!"

With revelation, TQ said, "Yeah, real peaceful."

Fred held out his hand and said, "Welcome to God's family, son."

TQ quietly replied, "No one ever called me son that I can remember. May I call you Dad?"

Fred studied Anne's face a moment and said, "After looking at my daughter, I'd say it's appropriate. Welcome to our family, son."

TQ stuck out his hand, but Fred grabbed him in a big hug TQ just had to give back. Then it was Paul's turn. Finally, gently, Anne slid her arms around his neck and kissed him in front of her father and god-father.

It was Paul, the ever-efficient agent, who broke the moment, "We have another prayer warrior on our side. Let's use it and get some rest before recon! It's almost ten minutes after eleven now."

TQ excitedly announced, "I don't think I could sleep."

Fred smiled and said, "Oh, you'll sleep. You'll sleep like a baby in his momma's arms. You'll be in God's arms."

Paul made a point with, "One thing to remember. People will fail you. Don't judge them too harshly or you will be judging yourself. Look for Christ in all things. Ask what he wants to teach you in both the good and bad situations. The enemy is subtle. He'll sneak up on you in little things. He's always after the man, the leader of the house. I know from experience. I failed, but I'm forgiven. That's the only difference between where you were and where you are now. Remember that!"

TQ firmly announced, "I will. Thanks! I didn't know I could be so blessed from a bomb explosion."

Fred, Anne, and Paul together said, "God works in mysterious ways!"

Everyone laughed.

Fred waved a hand in the air and said, "To bed, all of you. I've got first watch."

They were right. TQ was asleep almost from the moment his head hit the pillow. No bad dreams, no faces!

Three Miles Away

Doc Bailey and seven street wise veteran cops rehearsed the plans and options over and over again in the small rooms of the vacant motel.

Finally, Lt. Spence declared, "Enough! Load the vehicles with the weapons. Look to your personal gear. Get some sleep! I want everyone up and ready to go by 5:00 A.M. Doc, I still think you should wait in the wings and have a back-up take your place."

Doc answered his old friend, "Spence, I'm not one of those milk-toast doctors from the hospital. I did 'Nam' and made a career of patching you guys up. I seem to remember patching you up twice in the last seven years."

Spence resignedly answered, "Alright! Just stay down if it starts to rain lead."

Doc snorted as he patted the grip of the Colt Python pistol on his hip, "Like hell I will! I qualify every year. I've got my old Colt Python right here."

Spence asked again, "No way to change your mind, I suppose?"

Doc answered, "Nope! You need some of that shuteye, too. I'll take the first watch."

The squad dispersed! Doc pours a cup of coffee and thinks back to all his friends gone in the fight against wrong. It was a long list.

26

A Cord of Three Strands

At the Hotel

Ace was coming up the back stairs at the 14th floor when he heard a slight sound directly behind him. At the landing, he spun completely around to see a neatly dressed man with a bouquet of flowers smiling at him.

Flowers said, "Go right up. I can wait."

Ace generously offered, "You can go ahead. I'm in no hurry."

Flowers motioning for Ace to continue up retorts with a smile, "Hey, I get paid by the hour."

Ace continues up the stairs, turning his head and talking over his shoulder to cover his watchfulness of 'Flowers.' Each time he turned around, the smile on Flowers' face seemed larger.

Ace and Flowers entered the 16th floor together. Ace had just passed the door of the room beyond Mr. Peck's room when Flowers spoke, "Aren't you supposed to meet Manny about now?"

Ace turned to see Flowers disappear into Mr. Peck's room. He hurried to get in before the door could close.

Flowers spoke like a confidant to Mr. Peck, "He did a very good job at the marina. He even spotted me coming behind him on the stairs. Needs work, but he'll do."

Manny explained this way, "Ace, this is BJ. Never take anyone at face value. I had him check you out. I already knew you did well, or you wouldn't be here now."

Ace felt an ice cube slide down his back!

BJ took a small caliber Glock out of the bouquet of flowers and slid it back into his right jacket pocket. He held up the flowers and said, "Never forget the beauty of this world." He stuck out his hand and took Ace's in a firm, friendly grip.

Manny swept them both with a glance and informed them, "Neither one of you is as close to this as I am. You don't know what I know, the whole picture. Here's the way it adds up: 1. TQ gets tired of these killing fields and wants out. 2. The team panics and conjures up all sorts of nonsense. I may be wrong on this. 3. They call in help. Help they can dispose of and place the blame on. You (Points to BJ.), me, Rosalita, and Bruce. 4. Problem! BJ here bails early. Then, I bail. Only Toy knew I was out when I left. Precautions…always precautions!"

"That leaves me two problems. It's where you, BJ, and my Ace in the hole come in. 1.I have to call at 6:00AM to tell the team where TQ and his friends are. 2. I have to meet face-to-face with TQ before I do that. I have to know for sure."

"BJ will make the call if it goes south. Ace will back me up with an automatic weapon. I'm sure TQ will be reconning the area every so often, but not at specific intervals. We'll be out in the cold tonight boys."

"BJ and I are on the same page. He's going back to his flower shop permanently after this. I have several legitimate businesses that bring in more money than I'll ever need. I always wanted a little brother. I just never thought he'd be Hispanic! What do you say to formal education, hard work, brandy, and lots of pretty women!"

Ace tapped his chin with a finger and says, "Hummmmmmm. Let me think. When do we leave, big brother?"

Manny grinned and replied, "As soon as I face TQ we'll head to Boston. I'll be staying there for a while, waiting for a call. Here's the plan…"

27

Discoveries

Back at The Safe House

Just shy of 2:00 A.M., Spooky is awakened with a hand over his mouth. Cypher whispered, "Get your clothes on and carry your shoes. Quiet now!"

When the pair had entered the cold, snow filled night, Cypher turned to Spooky.

Cypher explained his actions this way, "Manny seemed to know too much. Toy doesn't seem to be all I want her to be as a leader. I'm pretty good as a pick pocket. I lifted both his cell phones. I added a little something before I returned them. I've been recording all evening. You listen, but I'll give you the bottom line first. Manny is out! He's not coming back. Toy is in love with the guy and meeting him in Boston after this goes down. She's out, too! I really don't understand what's happening here."

Spooky asked, "Can we listen to what he's saying right now?"

Cypher shook his head NO and said, "Lost him about three miles from here."

Spooky looked side to side and said to Cypher, "I'm getting a bad feeling, a real bad feeling. We better watch each other's backs in the morning. Stay close!"

Cypher replied, "Like a shadow! Do we tell the others?"

Spooky whispered a little too loudly, "Who? Bruce and Rose? Who cares? We were going to get rid of them anyway. Crimp will be on the sidelines. Ricco is a hot head. Tell him now and he'll start killing everyone, right now. Yes, I'll tell them. Timing is the thing with this. I haven't made up my mind about Toy. One side of me wants to hit her now. However, if Manny cares for her like you said, I almost hope she makes it to Boston. Besides TQ, Manny is the last person I'd want hunting my hide. Destroy that stuff after I listen and get some sleep. We have to be up in a little over two hours. Let's go back in. It's freezing out here!"

Toy slept like a baby! With all the problems weighing on her, she had slept like a happy child. Manny had said to come to him. Not to sleep with him, not for a holiday fling. This feeling was new. It was wonderful. If she had never been in love before, what was it? Control! Lust! She'd never do that again. It was early. She would just lay here and enjoy thoughts of what the future might hold.

28
Reaching Out

At 10:30 P.M., Special Agents Katherine Scott and Jim Fry were still at the motel, discussing the plan Paul had briefed them on at the marina. He said they were done, no longer involved. Thanks for the Intel and go home. Both agreed the plan sounded good if (with a capital IF) the bad guys didn't get there first. They both agreed they had to do something more.

They had gone back to recon the bad guy's safe house earlier. The two watched as the pretty black female got out of the Lexus and went into the house. There seemed to be too much activity in the house for planning and info gathering sessions. They were about to act! Jim and Katherine could almost feel the intensity in the dark, 100 yards away. The snow kept them from seeing all they wanted to, even with the special optics. What they did observe gave them enough insight to cause them worry.

Paul had been specific. He said, "Don't come back here." They had spent the last few hours discussing whether they should go against Paul's orders. The risks were immense from all angles. If someone got hurt or killed because they disobeyed, they would be in jail for the next hundred years!

In the end it was decided they would cruise back and forth on the main road between the truck stop and a furniture store parking lot. The span was some 3.5 miles. Their cover would hold if stopped, unless someone spotted all the hardware they were packing. It was decided they would be on the road about 5:00 A.M.

Katherine was getting ready for bed and her thoughts turned to Paul. "If that man does something stupid and gets hurt, I'll kill him myself." She stopped with her hair half down and thought, "That doesn't make sense…unless I love that man! Yes, I do love that man! God, protect him. I need him alive! What do I do, God?'

29
Confrontation!

A little after 2:00 A.M., TQ's eyes popped open. He felt refreshed and ready. Ready for what? He stopped right then to say, "God, I know you're here. I'm not sure how to talk to you or if there are specific times you take calls. God, I'm asking for Your help to get myself and my new family, the one you gave me, out of this jam. You know I'm tired of killing. Maybe Anne is right! Just use me as a soldier. Thanks God."

TQ slipped into his clothes; dark jacket, skull cap, gloves and all his weapons. He tiptoed into Anne's room without a sound. As he bent to apply this new tradition to her cheek, her hand grasped the back of his head and she gently kissed him full on the mouth.

Anne laughed softly at his surprise and said, "What's the good in a tradition if you don't both enjoy it?"

TQ replied, "Don't forget that tradition when I return."

Anne sighed and said, "I'll be right here."

TQ slid out the side door of the garage and flattened himself against the wall to let his eyes and ears adjust to the night. What a night! The sky was clear and the stars were like diamonds in the black velvet sky, but lots more snow was on its way.

He was startled when the snow bank by the neighbor's garage whispered, "Don't look here. You're being watched. I came out about fifty minutes ago to recon when I spotted them moving in on us. I got this far and couldn't get in. They were very intent on getting here before you came out. I heard one ask a guy, a big guy like you, named Manny, if they should surround you and take you down. This Manny gave orders to stay back. He wants to confront you himself. The other two only act if you come out on top." "I've an idea. If you agree, just start moving. If you don't, blow into your hands and we'll work out another plan. Here it is."

"Head out to the street, but close to the houses like you are checking out the area. About halfway down the block head for the docks and boats dry-docked across the street. They'll be trying to follow you. If you feel up to it, just turn around when you reach the other side and call the guy out without a name. They'll think instinct or something warned you. I'll close in on the other two while they are glued to you. I should be able to effectively discourage one, maybe both, of the other two from their evil ways without noise or bloodshed. We will need information."

TQ bent and made a snowball he tossed toward the snow bank. He moved quietly toward the front of the house and the street. He took all the normal precautions when moving. He was wondering about the three men closing in on him. He was trusting in God and Paul Stanton. He knew Paul being stuck out here was no coincidence. He felt a lump come to his throat. A man he met less than six days ago was putting his life on the line for him. "Family…Thank God for family!" Quickly, TQ crossed from the shadows of one house to another. One, two, three houses! Now is the time! Let's head this off! A quick sprint to the dry-docked boats and spin around.

TQ loudly announced, "They call me the Ghost. You do pretty well yourself. How are you on guts? Step right out there in the middle of the road and the beautiful starlight so we can see each other. Bring anything to the game you want. I don't think you're good enough!"

A half a breath after the challenge was dropped, a handsome, rugged black man, almost as big as TQ, materialized between two houses. He purposefully walked to the center of the street. He turned his back on TQ and stripped himself of his jacket, skullcap, three guns and a knife that he piled neatly on the ground. Then he walked about ten feet back toward the cottage and stopped to face TQ. This was obviously to put himself closer to his backup.

TQ couldn't help grinning when he thought of the surprise Manny's back up would be having. Strange though, he had heard that Manny always worked alone!

TQ chided, "Well, Mr. Manny Peck! I never thought you would be a part of this kind of treachery! Two questions! Are they paying you well? Have you named a beneficiary to spend it? I can't say it's nice to finally meet you."

Manny pointed to the pile in the street and announced, "I'm unarmed except for what I am."

TQ said, "I may be crazy, but I believe you."

TQ removed his coat, skullcap, and weapons. He piled them as neatly as Manny on the side of the road. He flexed and felt the joy of combat rushing through his warrior veins. This is a worthy opponent. Win or lose, it will be one heck of a battle!

TQ couldn't help speaking out loud, "God, Your will be done!"

Manny was waiting, confident, until he heard TQ say that. For the first time ever a feeling of doubt, like wiggling worms, settled into the pit of his stomach. He tried to shake it off as TQ walked toward him with catlike grace and a huge grin. Manny knew he would have to stop TQ before he could even talk to him. Stop him, or maybe be killed by him.

No more was said. Both attacked furiously like two tigers claiming the same territory. The sounds of flesh on flesh, grunts, and labored breathing was accented by the sweat pouring out of muscles, exerting pressure against pressure, strength against strength, even in the extreme cold. TQ got a kick to the center of Manny's chest that pushed all the air out in a rush as he was propelled back into the snow. As TQ tried to follow up, Manny caught him coming in with his feet and flipped him into the curb at the edge of the street. TQ shook his head and was rising to meet his opponent when he saw Manny already up, backing away slowly, holding his chest with his left hand.

Manny asked, "You beat up enough to stop and talk awhile?"

TQ incredulously answered, "Me? You aren't looking through my eyes! What's this about talk?"

Manny threw back, "That's eye! Singular! Your left one's about swelled shut. Damn, you are good! I'll give you that."

TQ relaxed a little and said, "You're not so bad yourself. Talk!"

Manny confidently explained, "I didn't come here to kill you. If I had, I could have popped you while you were leaning against the house back there. Besides, you couldn't win. This time I didn't come alone. You were in the cross-hairs of my two associates the whole time."

Right then, Manny's Lexus SUV came around the corner without lights and stopped next to the two men. On the hood were the inert forms of two men, bound and gagged like trophies after a successful hunt.

TQ chuckled and said, "I see. And, where would you like your associates to be for the ride home? Does my associate untie them so they can ride in warmth and comfort or would you rather they stay where they are?"

Manny couldn't help himself. First, he grinned, then chuckled, then burst into a full-throated laugh which had him holding his bruised ribs and chest. TQ and Paul were soon following suit; much to the chagrin of Ace and BJ, still tied to the hood of the Lexus.

Manny looked at TQ and said through the laughter and pain, "If I knew you were so much fun, we'd have done this years ago! Can we get our coats now? It sure is wicked cold out here! Unless, of course, you want me to beat on you some more!

TQ held up one hand and said, "I don't think either of us could take much more."

Manny resignedly answered, "I don't want to admit to that, but I will say it would be counter-productive. By the way, how did that guy get out without us spotting him?"

TQ glanced at Paul and said, "Some things are best left as mysteries. Paul, let them loose."

Paul cut their hands free and backed up to watch the two men struggle out of the ropes and off the hood of the Lexus. The two men looked at Paul, then to Manny Peck.

Manny pointed to Paul and said, "One at a time, go and introduce yourselves to the gentleman, then to TQ. Don't mess with either. I wouldn't be much help and I've pretty well found out what I came for. TQ isn't going to turn anyone in. He just wants out!"

BJ, with wounded pride, asked, "How'd you figure that out, from getting pounded to a pulp? No offense, of course."

Manny held his ribs and replied, "None taken. Here's your lesson in logic for this evening. If TQ was planning on ratting out anyone, you two would be dead, not tied to the hood of the Lexus. Plain and simple Doctor Watson!"

Ace pointed to Paul, "Never saw him, never heard him. All I saw was stars. My head hurts!"

Manny, with a studious look at Paul, said, "He is or was military, Rangers or Special Forces, I suppose. They never lose the movements!"

Paul looked at TQ, then back to the other three, "What now?"

TQ asked Paul, "Anne made a chocolate mayonnaise cake, didn't she?"

"You ate about half of it," retorted Paul

TQ looked at Manny, "What do you say to cake, coffee, and conversation?"

Manny looked at his watch before he replied, "We have about three hours. It's almost three now. I'll explain over cake and coffee. This Anne, she a good cook? BJ, drive us there in the Lexus. I hurt too much in too many places to walk very far."

30
New Friends

The noise of boisterous males in the kitchen at three in the morning prompted Anne to don a robe and investigate. After a quick, short prayer for safety, she hurried into the kitchen, a gun in her robe pocket. Three strange men with her dad and Paul had stopped eating long enough to appreciate her beauty and mumbled how good the cake was before continuing their arduous task of eating large quantities of cake between slow sips of hot coffee. The tall black man seemed to be having a very difficult time chewing. He looked like he had been in a horrible fight! Where was TQ?

Just then, TQ's now familiar touch fell on her shoulders and his lips tenderly kissed her right cheek. Anne could feel something was wrong and fairly whirled around to face him.

Anne gasped, "Ohhh, TQ! What happened? Let me fix you up!"

TQ smiled and said, "I'm fine. I heal really quick! I got this when I bumped into a new friend."

Anne threw a scolding look at Manny.

Manny held up both hands and said, "Hey, I didn't get off Scott free! Your boyfriend can handle himself pretty well!"

Anne would have gotten a light shade of red only a few days ago. Now, she just smiled and said, "As I am sure you are well aware. Now, who is going to fill me in? No one leaves this kitchen until I have answers."

Fred interjects, "Honey, I'm waiting for those same answers. I think we'll get them shortly. They've eaten all the cake and most of the leftovers."

TQ interjected, "I think we are going to need the table for maps and a lot of coffee. I'll get the maps."

Fred offered, "I'll get the coffee. I've a feeling Anne should get dressed."

Anne crossed her arms defensively and announced, "After someone tells me what is going on."

Manny filled her in, "Ma'am, I'm Manny Peck. This is Ace, and this is BJ. We were told that TQ was going to put us out in the open, turn us over. We were recruited by his old *Team* to help hunt TQ down and eliminate him. We never met, but I have a file on him as thick as my fist. Nothing fit, it just wasn't his style. He has class and that is definitely not class. I had to make sure for myself. We have a problem. I gave my word that I would call and tell them where TQ is at 6:00 A.M.. Now, don't get upset! I never said I would tell them how to get to him or anything like that."

Ace murmured, "It's snowing again. It's nice just being in here."

BJ concurred, "Yeah!"

Manny spoke to the two men, "Sorry guys! We can't stay and help them. I gave my word I was going to Boston to meet a very special lady."

TQ spoke up, "Toy is special. She just never thought so herself. Don't hurt her!"

Manny emphatically announced, "Never!"

Paul, looking at dials on a black box, declared, "You're broadcasting!"

Incredulous, Manny asked, "What?"

Paul repeated, "You're sending out some kind of signal. My equipment doesn't lie."

Manny off-handedly replies, "Oh, probably just my cell phones. We have clean ones."

Paul sternly said, "I'm an Intel tech, among other things. You're sending! Where are those phones?"

Manny handed Paul the phones.

Ace watched over Paul's shoulder as he deftly opened each phone and pointed out the devices. He puts his finger to his lips and pointed to the faucet. Fred turns on the faucet. Paul set the phones on the sink and motioned everyone into the living room.

Paul said, "That should do it. You want to tell us what that is all about?"

Manny and TQ exclaimed together, "Cypher!"

Manny continued, "I thought Cypher was getting a little close a couple of times. I never felt him lift them or put them back. What kind of bugs are they?"

Ace said, "I've seen them before. They are audio transmitters, digital, and very clear. They don't go too far. If you are more than a couple of miles from the receiver they lose the signal. I've got clean phones in the back of the Lexus."

Manny tersely ordered "Good! Get them and be back in here quick."

BJ asked, "What's the matter Manny?"

Manny asked TQ, "If Cypher was listening, would he be recording?"

TQ nodded, "Always!"

Manny, a little franticly, announced, "They know Toy wants out! She's in there by herself and doesn't even know it. She was to meet me in Boston."

Anne quietly stated, "I'll take it that you've changed your mind about leaving."

Manny, just as quietly, answered, "I've got something special to stay for, now."

Fred took command, "It's almost four. Soldiers need an hour or two sleep, to bed! I'll take first watch." He pointed to Ace. "I'll wake up junior there in one hour. Paul will take 6:00 A.M. BJ will start at 0700 hours. Anne, I hate to say it, but you have to be up by six and have breakfast ready by 6:30. Everyone to bed! We all need what rest we can get." He looked at the three newcomers. "If you are praying people, do it! If not, start!"

They all headed off to find places to sleep.

Paul stopped abruptly and said, "Whoa! Are we all so tired that we forgot about Doc!"

Fred retorted, "Nope! I'll explain in about two hours. Get some rest."

31
Dawn of Trouble

At 4:30 A.M., Doc and his team were up and going over all the details one last time. Breakfast would be in a half hour. They would move out at the direction of Fred Donner. They were waiting for the call. If this went bad, they could all kiss their pension's good-bye, maybe their lives.

At the Safe House
Spooky decided Toy had to go, for self-preservation. They would take their chances with Manny Peck. Maybe the team would visit him in Boston one last time. Spooky should have been the leader. He wasn't just telling himself he should have taken over the team. He told Cypher, and was recruiting Ricco now. Rosalita would be easy. She thought Toy was too pretty. She would be next. The others would fall in line as soon as Toy was out of the picture. He just wasn't sure about Crimp. No one except TQ could read the guy.

Toy would not be suspicious if he woke the team up now, 4:30 A.M., to make sure they were all ready to roll. She would be up in a half hour or so anyway. First, Rosalita so she could make breakfast, prepare something special for Toy. Then, Ricco would be next. He'll want to act right away. Might have to sit hard on him for a while! Last, would be Bruce. He has no loyalty to any of the team. Bruce would bend to the way the wind was blowing.

Spooky got the team up in order. Then, he put the final part of his leadership takeover into action.

Alone in the kitchen, Spooky told Rosalita, "Rosalita, when you fix breakfast make Toy's special. Send her off as quietly as possible."

Rose crossed herself and said with a smile, "The pretty one will be sleeping in the lap of Jesus this morning."

5:30 A.M., Toy couldn't believe it. Everyone else was done eating breakfast when she arrived at the table. Ricco was already outside with Bruce.

Spooky explained, "I sent Ricco and Bruce out to get two SUVs ready to go. Figured we should leave the hummer here to transfer to after the operation. I think we should torch the place when we leave. No evidence is the best evidence!"

Toy pat Spooky's shoulder and said, "My plan exactly! Good work!"

Cypher got up from breakfast and announced, "Rosalita outdid herself. No telling when we'll sit down and eat like this again."

Bruce, coming in from outside, said to Crimp, "Yeah, and you are the bloody last one to the tucker. That's food to you uneducated blokes."

Crimp replied, "We knew what it was! Where did you ever get a word like tucker, anyway?"

Bruce ignored the comment and said, "You're driving the second vehicle. We have to go over the routes, alternates, etc. We also have to check weapons. You ready to move? I have a man with a vehicle to swap and a way to get us into Canada less than two hours after we notify him."

This was planned by Spooky and Bruce to get Crimp out of the way when Rosalita fed Toy her breakfast.

Spooky directed, "Dress warm, it's only 10 degrees out there. It's 5:40 A.M. We will leave in ten minutes."

Toy was over half done with her breakfast as she looked up and said,

"We're not to leave until after six. I'm waiting for a call. We'll be there five minutes and then we are out of here!"

Suddenly, she was very hot and wiped sweat from her forehead as the first pain hit her stomach.

Spooky took in the ashen color creeping into Toy's face and spoke frankly, "Toy, you sold us out, you and Peck. We don't need Peck's Intel to find them. We've narrowed it down already. You're not going with us to hit TQ. You're not going anywhere!"

Rosalita, smiling, quipped, "Hope you enjoyed my special breakfast, pretty one."

Toy knew she had been poisoned, how or why she did not know. She sprang from her chair as pain hit her stomach again and put her fork through Rosalita's jugular with a fatal twist.

Rosalita grabbed her throat as if to stop the bleeding. The blood flowed down her dress as Rosalita slowly sank to the floor.

Spooky was stunned. He never thought Toy would have the strength left to react like that.

In the few seconds this took place, Toy had bolted out the door. It was very cold, snowing pretty hard, and she was dying of poison. It would be hard to find her in the snow. Looking would throw off the timetable. If they could find her when they got back from the hit, they would throw her in the house with Rosalita and cremate both of them at once. If not, the government would find them and clean it up anyway. They don't want bad press. Man, this was all falling apart! Spooky got one of his bad feelings. "Aw Crap!" was all he said as he opened his first beer of the day. He calmly stepped over Rosalita's body and turned off the burner on the stove.

Out loud, Spooky said, "Damn you, TQ!"

Cypher entered the kitchen with all their AWOL bags. He dropped Rose's bag on the floor next to her and asked, "Where's Toy? I thought she would be the one lying there."

Spooky replied, "Turning into an ice cube about now. Let's go!"

Where Is Doc

Doc listened as Lt. Spence told him the ambulance had a flat. The snow was falling heavy. Visibility was limited. It would set them back fifteen, maybe twenty minutes.

Doc picked up a cell phone and punched a couple of buttons. The phone at the other end rang.

Fred answered the cell phone, "Saw your number Doc. What's up?"

Doc candidly replied, "Fifteen to twenty-minute delay. Bad sneaker!"

Fred said, "Not good, but we'll make do. We're three more now; a real *Team* of our own."

Doc sighed and told Fred, "I'm not going to ask. You fill me in later. See you soon."

Fred threw back, "Make it soon, real soon!"

Fred had very little sleep, about an hour. His adrenaline was flowing heavy. His emotions like those in Vietnam. Instead of heat, there was cold. Instead of lush vegetation, there was snow. Both were hostile. He was ready.

It was only 5:40 A.M., but everyone had already returned to the kitchen.

Paul had taken to the kid, Ace. They were dressed to go out to recon. He was going to show Ace how to become invisible in the snow and how to move without making crunching noises in the snow. Nowhere was there a sign of fatigue! Everyone was ready. Anne had made scrambled egg sandwiches with bacon for everyone. There was lots of coffee. TQ and Manny took up most of the table with maps and sketches Manny made of Rosalita and Bruce. The sketches weren't the quality Jim produced, but they were recognizable.

BJ had found a roll of light wire in a garage next door. He was looking through drawers like they contained buried treasure.

Anne demanded, "What are you looking for, BJ?"

BJ mumbled, "Something that makes lots of noise."

Anne waved her left hand and said, "Mrs. Fulton, two doors down that way, is a wind chime collector. Check her back porch."

BJ grabbed his weapon, wire, pliers and left the house. It was 5:50 A.M.

Outside, Paul handed Ace the sheet. It was white, queen size.

Paul said, "You have a knife, right. Good! Cut holes for your eyes about here. Now, refold it and tuck it into your coat. Not that way! It has to open quickly, without a hang up. Don't zip your coat up all the way. If you have to disappear, get near a snow bank or snow-covered bushes. Don the sheet, squat, and don't move. They'll only see you if you move, especially in this snow. Watch!"

Ace watched as Paul took a few steps back toward the house they were next to, donned the sheet and squatted next to a snow-covered bush. If he hadn't just seen him do it, Ace would not have believed there was anyone there. Amazing! Ace tried it. It took him twelve seconds.

Paul demanded, "Again!"

They went through the drill four times before Paul was satisfied. Ace had it down to five seconds. Then he froze as he looked past Paul.

Ace declared, "Two vehicles coming. Big motors! They're probably SUVs!"

Paul pointed and said, "Cross the street there, run back between those two boats and gear down. Vanish!"

Ace was gone without a word.

Paul moved between the two houses and disappeared into the snow. He pushed the quick dial on the cell and stuck it into the snow bank.

32
Hell Coming Home

Inside the cottage, Fred's cell phone rang. Fred grabbed the phone, "Fred here."

Nothing, no wind, no voices! Fred shouted a warning as he turned off the lights, "They're here!"

TQ flipped up the couch. The chairs followed as Manny hit the other lights and grabbed weapons.

Fred turned over the kitchen table and the refrigerator quickly followed it, half the contents rolling across the floor. Father and daughter huddled together, unconsciously grasping each other's hand in the dark. Each had an automatic weapon in the other hand.

Manny, voice low, said, "Here's some backup."

TQ felt the unmistakable shape of a military frag grenade pressed into his hand. His admiration for his new friend was growing in leaps and bounds. Not only could Manny fight, he could think ahead.

A whooshing sound and suddenly the garage exploded, taking that part of the kitchen wall with it. A large fireball followed the explosion, blocking any exit there. The *Team* was making sure no one left. AK-47 automatic rifles, a shotgun, and other weapons were pouring lead in from three sides. Manny tapped TQ and pointed to the fourth side.

TQ nodded and watched Manny use the available cover to avoid the bullets flying through the room.

As Manny was crawling down the short hall, Anne's bedroom door slowly started to open. The muzzle of an automatic rifle appeared. Almost instantly the muzzle flashed and Manny felt a searing pain along his right hip. The shots were too fast, too wide. Manny spaced his shots about six inches above the floor, left, right, and center. He followed up with three more about twelve inches above the first three. The automatic tilted down slightly and fired twice into the floor in front of Manny. Splinters from the floor struck Manny in the face, luckily missing his eyes. The 'thunk' of the automatic rifle being dropped went unheard in the roar of the surrounding fire-fight. TQ's old *Team* was shooting and moving. They had that advantage.

Manny wiped away the blood that flowed into his left eye from a splinter wound on his forehead and crawled to the bedroom door. At first the door wouldn't give when he pushed. Then he put his massive body and strength behind the next shove and the body on the other side slid easily aside and the door moved inward. He reached Crimp as Crimp was breathing through bubbles of blood.

Crimp confessed, "It was no good. I knew it when they poisoned Toy. She ran out into the snow. Dead by now! Do you think hell is as bad as they say?"

His head tilted to one side. He was gone to whatever fate God had for him.

Thoughts ran through Manny's head, "Toy! Toy gone! No! No, not now! God, if you are half what these people believe, show me. Show me and I'll believe and serve you. Save Toy for me. Please God, please!" He hadn't learned yet God is always in control, always ahead of us.

Manny grabbed three clips and the automatic rifle off Crimp and dove through the open window into the snow outside. He tucked his automag into his waistband and reached into his right pocket for the round cold death of the frag grenade.

The shooting was confused now. The *Team* suddenly realized they were also targets, caught in a crossfire. Bruce, hit in the right forearm, was trying to reload a shotgun with one arm and heading for a vehicle. Cypher, bleeding from wounds in both legs, was struggling toward the other SUV when the snow in front of him erupted and a knife swung toward his throat. He flung himself to the side at that moment and the knife sliced cleanly through his cheek and ear, but missed anything vital.

Ricco and Spooky stopped firing and ran between houses as bullets from the docks tossed the snow around them into the air. This was a disaster! Retreat was in order! Training and discipline took over.

Manny spotted them running between cottages and turned to give chase before the falling snow covered their retreat. His feet stopped suddenly and he took a nose dive that ended after sliding on a face already tore up by splintered wood and TQ's fists. Before he came to a stop, somebody dropped on his back and a gun muzzle was pressed to the back of his head. It was BJ.

BJ apologized, "Sorry Manny! I thought I had one alive to talk to. Spooky and Ricco got away for sure, now."

Manny jumped up and shouted, "BJ, we have to get a vehicle and find Toy. She's been poisoned and is out in the snow someplace. Come on!

.

33
Close Encounters

Bruce reached the SUV, opened the driver's side door, and stared at the white ghost with the automag pointed at him for less than a second before he fired almost point blank and felt the punch of a bullet in his own chest, high and right. The ghost was gone and if he didn't get help soon, he would be, too.

Bruce had the SUV moving between two cottages almost as soon as it started. Left down the street, then right toward the main road! He almost hit the ambulance and cop cars coming at him. Then, he almost spun out of control trying to avoid hitting Ricco and Spooky when they jumped into the road. He slammed it into reverse as the two jumped into the moving SUV. The tires howled as he threw it into drive.

Spooky asked, "Hit bad?"

Bruce nodded, "Need a Doc."

Spooky ordered, "Pull over. I'll drive while Ricco patches you up. He knows something about it. We have to get the Hummer and torch the house."

Ricco, working on Bruce, asked, "What about Toy?"

Spooky replied, "You want to wait around looking for her body? I'm out of here."

Ricco balled his fists and said, "I'm pissed! This isn't over. I'll find him! I'll find him!"

Bruce felt the pain in his bloody wounds and agreed, "Yeah, me too. What about you?"

Spooky answered them both, "I think we are trapped into it, no choice."

Bruce suggested, "Let's go to my place. They'll never find us there. We can come back when we're ready."

No more was said. Escape was the first priority.

Doc and his crew almost hit the SUV head-on. Were they too late? They could see the glow of flames through the falling snow. All was quiet as they slid to a stop in front of the burning cottage. Immediately, a large black man, Manny, with an air of command, pulled the driver of one car out and shoved another man into the driver's seat.

Manny spoke as one in charge, "Tell TQ we went to the safe house. They poisoned Toy. Move over, I'm coming in!" In less than eight seconds, the police car was going back the way it had come with two strangers and three of Doc's police officers.

At that moment, Fred, Anne, and the mystery man were heading toward Doc. Suddenly a shout of 'Medic' broke the stillness and Doc sprang into action. He found Paul, a friend of Fred, sitting in the snow holding a bloody young man cradled in his arms. Was Paul crying? The young man was unconscious and barely breathing. A quick once-over told Doc he wasn't hit too badly, but was bleeding out.

Doc ordered, "Give me his wallet!"

Doc rifled through the cards in the wallet until at last he exclaimed, "Yes! Yes! Don't worry about being gentle. Speed boys! Hurry, I've got blood in the ambulance. Move!"

Katie and Jim had taken hours to prepare and plan. They still did not have a concrete plan to assist their friends. They finally decided on the direct approach. They parked the car when they got close enough to see the glow of the fire, and people moving around like shadows through the snow. They were a block away, moving cautiously toward the scene.

Cypher had stopped crawling long enough to slow the bleeding on his face. He tied a handkerchief to his face with a sleeve he tore from his shirt. Then, he crawled toward the road. He had to get out of there. He was sure Bruce had made it out, maybe others. He had to find a way to get to the safe house before they left.

The two people, guns in front of them, were so intent on the activity at the burning cottage they passed within six feet of Cypher and never noticed him sitting quietly in the falling snow. As soon as they passed him, Cypher struggled to his feet and made his way to the vehicle the two had just left. What great luck, the keys were in the ignition! As Cypher sped off toward Bruce and the hummer he exclaimed, "Thank you, idiots!"

34
Is Toy Dead?

Toy had bolted through the kitchen door into the biting cold and the snow. But now she was doubled over with pain coming in waves. She jammed a finger down her throat and threw up as much of what was in her stomach as possible. She moved, fell, struggled up, and repeated this until she couldn't do it anymore. Toy thought she had gone a long way when she finally collapsed. In truth, Toy had covered only about sixty-five feet. She lay still in the snow; not feeling the cold, only the pain – the pain! She lost consciousness.

Toy didn't know what brought her back at first. It was heat, intense heat. The house was burning. She felt the pain, the cold, the heat, and passed out again.

BJ, Manny, and their newly acquired police force stopped in the driveway a couple of hundred feet from the burning house. Manny ran around the house looking into the flames. Maybe Toy was in there! What did Crimp say? Snow! Snow, that's it! Toy is out in the snow somewhere. She had to be! BJ and Manny had been too close behind Bruce and the others for them to find Toy. They didn't have time to throw her into the burning house. Where? Where?

The bleeding didn't stop. Cypher was lightheaded from loss of blood.

He was making it. There's the house. It's burning. He had to pass this cop car and go to the barn to meet Bruce. They had to be there, just waiting for him.

Cypher crashed the barn door just as Spence and his two officers dove out of his path. He kept driving through the open barn doors at the other end, missed the turn onto the logging road, and was abruptly stopped by a very large oak tree. He lay over the steering wheel staring at eternity and a short life full of misdeeds disguised a patriotic-acts. Who would mourn him? Who loved him? Who even knew him? Cypher closed his eyes as the velvet blackness took him, just as Officer Spence forced the door open. He never heard the policeman exclaim, "Oh God!"

Toy was floating. She heard a voice like Manny's say, "She's been poisoned, Doc. She's been out in the cold for over a half hour. I can't understand why she's still alive."

Doc tried to reassure Manny by saying, "If she threw most of it up before it got to her bloodstream we may have a slight chance the save her. The cold would slow her metabolism. Get her into the ambulance next to the kid. You squeeze in, too. That face needs real attention and there is blood on that hip! TQ looks like he had much the same experience. He was awful worried about you."

The medics were working on Toy even before Manny climbed into the ambulance. Luckily, Toy passed out once more before they put tubes down her throat and into her stomach.

Doc murmured, "One lunkhead worried about another lunkhead!"

Manny couldn't help but smile at the comment.

Manny confided, "Doc, if Toy doesn't make it, they'll wish they had all died right here."

Doc pursed his lips, then said, "I can't quote chapter and verse like Fred, but somewhere in the Bible it says, 'Vengeance is mine says the Lord!' It's human nature to want an eye for an eye and a tooth for a tooth. We want to play God! What will it cost you? What's the price? Think on it awhile."

Manny sat without a sound or movement while a medic pulled several slivers of wood out of his face and patched him up. One had been dangerously close to his left eye. He kept watching Toy breathe. Each time Toy had a flinch from pain, Manny would start to sweat. He squeezed his big hands together and whispered, "Please, God!"

The ambulance swerved and came sliding to a halt. Manny thought they must have had a near accident. Suddenly, the doors opened and an army of white coats swarmed over the ambulance. They had reached the hospital.

Manny was shocked to realize he hadn't been aware of his surroundings. He thought aloud, "This must be love. I even knew what was happening when I was shot over in the Ukraine. Do I really care for her that much? If I do, then, I must change. She must change. Change into what? How do we become normal? What is normal? I'm going to find out, right after I pay them back!"

The nurse taking his blood pressure glanced quickly at his face, just once, and sighed greatly. She had dark hair sprinkled with gray from twenty-one years of repairing people who looked a lot like this.

Manny had a feeling like he had just cursed in front of a nun. He started to get off the table.

Doc grabbed Manny's arm and said, "Sit down young man! You look like you should be in one of these rooms. Better still, come with me. The coffee in the cafeteria is terrible. It's just what you need to keep your mind off her for a minute or two. Come on, Doc's orders!"

35
Clean Up

When the bullets had stopped coming through the cottage, TQ turned to grab Anne's hand and leave the burning cottage. He found her and Fred scooping family albums, pictures, and family heirlooms into waste baskets.

Fred shouted, "They must be saved from the fire!"

TQ shouted back, "We need to leave now!"

Instead of leaving, TQ grabbed Grandma's quilt off the couch and started filling it like a large sack. Anne looked at him with tears of thanks in her eyes, then, hurriedly grabbed a picture of her grandparents off an end table. In the seconds before they finished, the fire became unbearable. It was impossible to get out the door. TQ handed the quilt bag to Fred. He picked up an easy chair as easily as the quilt and ran through the large front window with it. Before he could rise from the ground, the quilt bag was flying at him. TQ instinctively caught the quilt bag. Ann came next with two waste baskets. Fred quickly followed with a waste basket and an old briefcase as the ammunition left in the kitchen started to explode. The bullets hummed around them like angry bees.

TQ shouted, "Get down, now!"

The frag grenade he left by the couch exploded as they hit the ground. It sent shards of metal and flaming debris in all directions. An officer in the yard went down hard. He was obviously hit hard by something in that short exploding firestorm.

"Paul! Paul!" It was a voice Paul recognized as Katie's.

Paul curtly asked, "What are you doing here? I tried to keep you out of harm's way! Are you trying to give me a heart attack?"

Katie was about to reply as abruptly in her most professional voice when she paused and asked almost in a whisper, "You wanted to keep me out of harm's way? Why?"

Katie could have sworn his face got redder than the glow off the burning cottage. It was a question Paul's heart had the answer to, but his mind wasn't ready to admit.

Instead, Paul demanded, "Where's Jim? Since you two are here, I'm putting you two both to work. Get gloves, tags and evidence bags. Take pictures before you touch anything. The fire is going to destroy most of the evidence. Get what you can."

Katie responded, "Yes, sir!" Then softly added, "Honey!"

Katie didn't think it was possible, but Paul got even redder in the face. She turned to find Jim with a hum on her lips and a bounce to her step. Amid this destruction she felt simply wonderful! Ah, there was Jim talking to Fred and a uniform. Paul didn't even holler about the car being stolen! Now, she laughed out loud.

Doc already had Ace receiving blood in the ambulance. Paul told Doc Manny and four others had gone to the Team's safe house to look for a downed woman.

TQ, looking like he belonged in the ambulance, popped his head in the door, "You have to move this to the safe house in a hurry. I already gave instructions to the driver."

Doc knew the two downed officers only had superficial wounds. A second ambulance would be here before theirs reached the main road. More uniforms, state and local law enforcement, were arriving.

Paul, ever efficient, was directing clean-up operations. He yelled, "Get that meat wagon rolling!"

TQ asked Anne, "What do I do now?"

36
Follow My Lead

Anne Donner, the police officer, slid her arm in his and said, "Make statements, answer questions as honestly as you can without divulging anything classified. I'll find us some coffee!"

TQ grinned and, with a sweeping gesture toward the heap of burning rubble the firemen were vainly trying to extinguish, exclaimed, "This isn't a new tradition, I hope!"

Anne quietly voiced, "I'll miss that cottage, but we saved the memories for our children."

All of a sudden, TQ couldn't speak.

Anne led him to a Sheriff's operation van that had just arrived. The long tedious process of law and order was about to begin. TQ smelled the coffee Anne had mentioned as he followed her into the police operations van.

Anne was already reaching for two Styrofoam cups. She spoke to the sergeant, "I'm a cop, too, and he's more important than both of us. We need coffee!"

The sergeant looked at their condition and expressed, "Go for it!"

Anne continued, "I'll be making a statement. He doesn't exist. Dead men can't write. You won't understand, so don't try. There are feds all over this. You'll be told what happened. Believe it and repeat only what you are told, nothing more! Tell the Sheriff to ask for Paul Stanton. He's running the show. We'll keep drinking your coffee until you get back. I can tell you what I'm allowed then."

The sergeant left to complete Anne's request.

Anne turned toward TQ in the cramped van to view a smile that took in all of TQ's soot smeared face.

Anne reconstructs the events, "My house burns down. We almost get killed. My clothes and hair are a mess. I smell like smoke. There you are grinning like the cubs just won the World Series!"

TQ swooped her into his arms and kissed her all over her sooty face and then on her lips.

He boasted, "I am so proud, no, blessed, to know you and be loved by you, Anne Donner. I'd do it again if I had to!"

Anne smiled back and challenged, "Not if I can help it! However, don't let me stop you from telling me how you feel. I'm a great listener."

So TQ did, over and over again until the deputy came back into the van.

Fred had found his old friend, Paul. He knew Anne was with TQ. They would do what was necessary. He hoped it was over. Fred would have been more relieved if they had them all, dead or alive. They just got word another of the team had died at the safe house. Jim Frey and two state troopers were headed that way to keep local police and fire chasers from destroying evidence. There won't be much, if any, evidence left. Fire cleans up pretty good!

Fred informed Paul about Toy, "Paul, they found a woman alive. Doc took her, the kid, and Manny to a hospital."

37
Patched Up

CID Agent Paul Stanton excitedly said, "Her I want to talk to! Find Katie and send her to me right away."

Fred continued his information, "No hurry! The woman was poisoned. Doc isn't sure if she'll make it or not."

Paul gave his old friend a slap on the back and some directions, "Go back to your place and get us clothes. Meet me at the hospital. We'll clean up there. If she wakes up at all, I have to get some answers from her. Have you seen BJ?"

Fred shook his head and said, "Nope! I'm not looking either. He helped us!"

Paul smiled and said, "The correct answer is, BJ who?"

Fred finished his information with, "I can't wait for a long hot shower. I'll bring you clean clothes to the hospital. They're at Samaritan."

Paul asked, "Can you get Katie first!"

Fred located agent Katherine Scott directing several uniforms in evidence gathering.

Fred waved a hand to get Katherine's attention, "Hey, Katherine!"

Katherine acknowledged, "Over here!"

Fred, pointing in Paul's direction, "There's a CID officer over that way. He says he needs your assistance immediately!"

SA Scott hurried toward CID agent Stanton. Her heart was beating in time with her running feet.

Upon her arrival, Paul said, "Glad you're here!"

Katie replied, "That's not what you said a little while ago."

Paul waved his hands back and forth in front of his chest and said, "Don't mix me up. I have to be at that hospital in case that Toy woman comes out of it. You take over. You know what to do. Here's a list of particulars I'm looking for. I must leave at once."

With a mischievous smile, Katie asked, "What about starting a little tradition of our own?"

Paul incredulously asked, "What, here, now?"

Katie simply said, "Why not?"

In a voice of surrender, Paul said, "A few days ago I could have come up with twenty reasons. They all escape me now. Come here!"

He kissed her long and gently.

Paul held her at arms length and said, "Remind me to stop and properly thank God that you're all right."

Katie replied, "I think you just did. We are both happy, you said it. Now, get going. I've got a handle on this place!"

38

Escape

Paul greeted the men at the hospital cafeteria, "Fred, Manny! How's she doing?"

Manny, worried and perplexed, said, "Doc was just out. He mumbled something about another superb animal. Then he said we could probably see her in about twenty minutes."

Fred added, "I've already posted a guard in her room and two outside of an empty room in the next wing. Diversion, you know."

Paul replied, "Good!"

Paul looked at Manny and asked, "I know you don't exist either. How about filling us in as much as you can? Until we find the others, I won't sleep right."

Manny closed his eyes and shook his head before he said, "You won't find them. Maybe, only maybe, TQ or I could. They'll just vanish. Maybe even plastic surgery! They could come back as priests, a hot dog vendor at a baseball game, anything. They will come back! They're egos have been stepped on hard. We were just lucky, but they don't know that. They don't know you, Paul. They do know TQ, Fred and Anne. These three have to vanish, too."

Paul offered, "I'll set it up with witness protection."

Manny smiled ruefully and spoke, "No offense, but I can tell you where your last five witnesses are with a computer and ten minutes to work on it. You leave that to TQ and me. We'll be able to get in touch with you when its safe or we need you."

Fred queried, "What's this we thing?"

Manny explained, "They'll be after me and Toy, if they find out she's alive. Besides, I have no family. I figure you'll make a great grandfather for my kids."

With a mock stiffness, Fred said, "Poppop is ok. None of that Grampy or Gramps stuff."

Laughingly, Paul asked, "Why? Does it sound too much like grumpy?"

Paul and Manny laughed as Fred tried his best to look angry while the corners of his mouth turned up in a grin.

Fred, with obviously false irritation, announced, "That's it! You two buy breakfast!"

Looking past Manny's shoulder with a shocked expression, Paul asked, "Hey, should he be up?"

Down the hall came Ace. He was inching his way along, steadying himself by leaning on the wall. His shoes weren't tied and his shirt was out. His bloody coat hung off him and bandages were visible on his head and left arm. There was a bulge under his shirt where a bandage was applied.

Ace haltingly whispered, "I came as soon as I could, Mr. Peck."

Manny spoke with gentleness in his voice, "It's Manny! You earned it, Ace. I'm real proud to have a little brother like you. Right now, we're getting you back in bed. There will be guards posted in and outside the room. No protests! I need you strong in less than a week. We're moving, five, six days, tops! Can you get well enough in that time?"

Ace tried to stand straight and said, "Sure, Manny. I sure can."

Manny caught Ace under the arms as he collapsed.

Doc came running up the hall with a nurse and a wheel chair.

Doc frantically asked, "How'd he get this far? Nurse, take this man back to his room. Hook him back up. I'll be right there to check on him."

Paul ordered, "Put some chairs in there. He'll have company his entire stay."

Fred stated the obvious to Manny, "You like that kid."

There was a tremor to his voice when Manny replied, "Never had a kid brother, even a Hispanic one."

The men chuckled as they turned toward the cafeteria. It was deserted because of the time of day and bad weather. It would be a good place to talk and plan over coffee that was worse than any the military had ever made.

39
Taking Flight

The hummer was parked next to a genuine UPS van. The driver was moonlighting for the moment as a livery for five thousand dollars. That's not bad for less than an hours work. It'll buy lots of presents for Christmas. He had called in with a flat as cover. Load the passengers and away we go. The driver commented, "Hey, don't bleed on the packages! How you been, Bruce? Long time no see!"

Bruce held his wounded arm and said, "Been better! You drop us off where I told you. Here's the money. You never saw us."

Exactly twelve minutes later, the van stopped alongside a large snow plow. The men climbed into the cab with a driver who looked like he had voted for Teddy Roosevelt for president. He never said a word. He plowed the road all the way to the Canadian border and turned around. Here he paused long enough to ask the Border Patrol Officer (BPO) in the SUV if he was stuck.

BPO answered, "No, Henry. We're looking for a bronze hummer. Seen one?"

Henry shouted over the noise of the big engine, "Nah, if I see it, I'll call it in."

BPO waved and shouted back, "Good man, Henry. Happy holidays!"

Henry waved back, "You, too!"

The three men had taken the opportunity to jump over the snow bank from the off side of the plow truck. There would be no visible tracks for the BPO to see.

About a half mile down the road, Henry reached over and pulled the passenger door all the way closed, patted the bulge in his coat pocket, and started singing *We Wish You a Merry Christmas*.

Spooky knew they needed Bruce. They were in the woods. He could kick himself for not going over the plan in detail with Bruce. They needed Bruce just to survive. Bruce was stumbling on the snow-covered path.

Spooky put his arm around Bruce and said, "Hold on Bruce. Lean on me. That's it. I'll help you."

Bruce in a thankful voice said, "Had you blokes figured wrong. You're turning out alright. We'll find TQ. Sooner or later, we'll find him. I want in all the way."

Ricco exclaimed, "Now you're talking! I hate that guy! If I ever get my sights on Manny Peck, I'll blow out his lights, too."

Spooky said nothing. He knew the emotion would help get them through, keep them moving.

Bruce suddenly straightened and asked, "How far have we come on this trail?"

Ricco shrugged and said, "About a half mile or so. It's hard to figure in the snow and the dark."

Spooky concurred by saying, "You're about right."

Bruce hastily asked, "See any stumps around here?"

Looking over his shoulder, Spooky said, "We just passed some. They're right behind us."

Bruce exclaimed, "We almost missed it! Go back. There, that one, the fourth stump. Reach behind it."

Ricco felt around behind the stump. "Plastic bag with a flash light!"

Bruce pointed due North and said, "Shine it right over that way. No, higher, waist high!"

The dull whine of snowmobile engines came to life. Lights began moving in their direction, one for each of the *Team*. That was more than they needed now.

Bruce indicated the two yellow sleds and said, "You two guys get on those sleds. The drivers will take you to a clean vehicle and a place to lay low."

Spooky asked, "Where are you going to be?"

Bruce wistfully replied, "Home! Actually, close to home. I have to make sure I'm not being hunted."

Ricco woodenly returned, "That sounds good to me!"

Bruce smiled thinly, "Follow the plan. Go where you will. If you need to see me or talk to me, there are the directions on this 3X5 card."

Spooky suddenly admired this man. He had considered him as inferior in the business. Bruce had stuck. He had pulled them out when he could have run them over with the SUV and gotten away.

Spooky held up the card and promised, "We'll let you know when we turn up TQ. I'm dedicating my life to it."

Ricco put a hand on a shoulder of each of the other men and said, "Yeah, we're like the three musketeers."

They followed the same trail for about five miles. Bruce raised a hand. The extra sleds and the one Bruce rode on veered to the left and disappeared into the snowy blackness. Spooky and Ricco were taken another eight or ten miles to a motel on the outskirts of a small Canadian town. The driver of Ricco's sled handed him a key and the two sleds left without a word.

Spooky voiced the plan as the made their way to the motel room, "We'll stay the night, maybe two. Then we'll head for warm weather, hot women, and anonymity."

Ricco nodded his approval and replied, "I like the way that sounds!"

40
Starting Over

During the next six days, Manny and TQ made plans. Manny realized TQ earned the name Ghost righteously. They had clothes, specific clothing, sent from different stores to locations only TQ and Manny knew about. They were paid for with money orders from different places on the East coast and sent to eleven different locations. TQ also made several dozen calls no one could understand. He spoke Navajo!

On day six, a squalid looking old lady with two shopping carts filled with what looked like old bottles and cans stopped next to Anne while she and two plainclothes officers were running an errand for TQ.

Old Lady asked Anne, "You got some money. I'll trade you all these for five dollars. I need some food."

Anne compassionately replied, "I'll give you ten. You keep your bottles."

Old lady took the ten spot and says, "Couldn't take this less you take the bottles."

As the old woman turned to go, Anne saw the two long black braids hanging to her waist outside her coat. At the corner, the old lady looked back at Anne and smiled. Suddenly, she was gone! She must have went around the corner.

After the errand, the two officers pushed the carts three blocks back to the hospital. They left them on the curb. Another homeless person would get them.

As soon as Anne saw TQ she said, "TQ, the strangest thing just happened…"

TQ cut in, "I see you met Morning Lilly. Did she smile at you at all?"

Anne replied, "Is that her name? Why, yes, she smiled just before she disappeared at the corner!"

TQ announced, "Good! Now we can be married!"

A little taken back, Fred asked, "What?"

TQ explained, "Morning Lilly was a medicine woman, an herbalist. No Hocus-Pocus, just good natural medicine. She saved my life a couple of times! She's the mother that I can remember."

Smiling, Anne said, "I like her already. When can I meet her?"

TQ shrugged and told the two uniformed officers, "Don't know. We'll see."

"You officers can go out, please. Thanks! Everyone else gather around and look at these pictures. This will be our new home."

As excited comments of lovely and beautiful were applied to the pictures, Manny suddenly exclaimed, "Wait a minute! We eat together, sleep together, we even go to the bathroom together sometimes. How'd you get those pictures?"

TQ smiled and made a waving gesture with his hands, "Magic!"

Everyone knew he would never tell them this secret.

Manny was particularly amazed by his new friend. He knew he was going to learn a lot from TQ. Dangerous! Sure was, but it was going to be a lot of fun, too.

Manny found out two things when they worked out together in the gym. He couldn't out fight TQ overall. But, capital BUT, in straight boxing he kicked his Indian butt all three times. That felt pretty good!

The door opened and Ace came in, straight and steady, but limping just a little on the left leg.

Manny hugged him and said, "Ace! Man, it's good to see you up and around. We weren't sure you were going to be well enough in time to go with us."

Ace returned with, "Me either. Funny thing though. Every night, starting the second night, this funny talking little nurse with long black braids would come in twice a night with medicine to drink. I slept really well! I felt good. The pain was gone by the fourth night. I was going to mention it, but Doc Bailey said not to tell anyone until I was up and around. He couldn't explain how I was healing so fast, either. He wasn't even sure how she got to my room. No one else saw her."

Everyone looked at Ace, then turned to look at TQ. A quick knock on the door took their attention.

Fred called, "Come in!"

An officer opened the door and Toy was wheeled in by Paul and Katie. Toy looking only at Manny asked, "Am I welcome at this party?"

Manny answered, "No party here. They're frivolous things!"

Toy agreed, "Good! I'm done partying."

Manny took two strides and lifted her from the wheelchair. He kissed her quick and said, "We can have private parties after we are married."

Toy giggled and said, "Often, very often, I hope!"

Anne broke in to say, "You look good, very good. Six days ago you looked like you were at death's door. How'd you recover so quickly?"

With a perplexed look, Toy replied, "It must have been the change in my medicine. I noticed it within two hours after taking the new medicine."

While looking toward TQ, Anne asked, "What medicine change?"

Toy answered, "I'm not sure. Twice each night this lovely old nurse with the prettiest long black braids would come in and give me the medicine. I don't think I need that wheel chair, but Doc Bailey insisted on it. It was the only way he'd let me out."

During this discourse, every eye turned to TQ.

TQ just smiled and said, "The Lord works in mysterious ways!"

He put a blank look on his face only a Native American can accomplish, unreadable, but a bright sparkle lit up eyes.

TQ spoke, "Paul, we all want to thank you and Katie, err Katherine."

Katie replied, "It's OK. I've learned to love Katie."

Speaking to Paul, TQ said, "Well that's great, huh Paul."

Paul looked at Katie and said, "Yeah! We're going to be married in Kentucky so her sister can be there. We sure wish all of you could be there, too."

Fred put his arm around his old friend and spoke for the group, "We will be there in spirit. Go with our blessing and love."

There was a time of hugs, kisses, and some tears all around. Then, Paul and Katie left hand in hand.

Without looking at his watch, TQ said, "In precisely three minutes and seven seconds there will be a disturbance that will draw attention from our door for about twenty-three seconds. That means we are out of the hospital side entrance in fifteen seconds. Start wiping down the place. I've already had the other three rooms and our hotel rooms taken care of. Ace, get those maps and papers. Put them in that bag. Get your coats on. We aren't stopping for a while. Go to the bathroom now if you have to. Make it quick! Toy, can you move fast enough?

Manny spoke as he lifted Toy off her feet, "I've got her!"

After grabbing a couple of small knapsacks, Fred said, "I've got the rest of our stuff. It isn't much at that. You already sent the things we saved from the fire ahead, right?"

With an air of command, TQ nodded, and then asked, "Ready? We'll wait four seconds after the ruckus starts. Fred first, then Ace, Manny and Toy, and last will be Anne and myself. A door will open to a panel van. Get in quick and move to the rear. Move quick without running. We want absolutely no attention."

Lots of loud noise and commotion began in the hospital lobby.

TQ counted, "One, two, three, go! Go now!"

The operation took all of nineteen seconds. The van door closed and it moved down the street with the rest of the traffic. The unknown driver never spoke or looked around.

41
Where Are Our Enemies?

Four days after the disastrous encounter with TQ and his new family, Bruce arrived in Australia. He gathered his family, gave them instructions, and left the same afternoon for an extended stay in the wild outback. He was hiding from ghosts that didn't exist.

Ricco and Spooky were unsure of their destination. Ricco finally gave in to Spooky's suggestion to go to Mexico. There they could recoup and recruit a new *Team*. They were out in the cold, disinherited from the US Government. That was ok with them. They had lots of opportunities in third world countries. Some party with money would pay to get person or persons out of their way; to clear a political agenda or settle a grudge. It would take a year, maybe more, to build up the treasury and recruit a team. Then, they would look for TQ. They would find him. They would kill him. They would show him how tough he was! Wheels were set in motion.

42
New Families

The trip for TQ's new family had been long, round about, but far from boring. The small Lear Jet landed on a dirt road in the desert just north of Gila, Arizona. TQ ordered, "Quiet." No words were spoken. Three old pick-up trucks appeared out of the rocks and stopped near the plane. Each had three young Native American men in the back of each truck armed with rifles which looked like extensions of their bodies.

TQ got out and approached the first truck. A gnarled old man with a black Stetson hat spoke to TQ. TQ seemed to give deference and respect to the old man. TQ came back to the plane and gave instructions. Everyone was to get out of the plane and line up in the order they exited the plane. They did as they were told. Somehow, they knew it was important.

When the old man got out of the first truck, the other drivers stayed with their trucks. The nine young men jumped out of their respective trucks and formed a semi-circle behind the old man. Each was dressed alike in old jeans, plaid shirts, and scuffed cowboy boots. Each man carried a well-kept rifle, each covering specific targets. The small group from the plane were well aware that they were the specific targets. When the first eight were in position, the man on the left had moved to take up a position where he could specifically watch the pilot of the plane. He trained his rifle at the pilot behind the cockpit window.

The pilot very carefully and slowly raised his hands and rested them on the top of the plane's instrument panel so the young Indian could see them.

TQ ordered, "Ace, Manny, take off your sunglasses."

The old Indian moved like a man in his thirties. He was obviously over seventy-five. His wrinkled face and slightly graying hair proclaimed wisdom and experience instead of age. He moved in front of Fred and stared into his face. Fred returned his look for a full ten seconds. The old man slapped Fred on the right shoulder twice and handed him an amulet of some kind.

TQ quietly explained what had just happened, "Fred, he has selected you to be his representative patriarch of our clan. You will ask him for counsel and meet with him twice a year, in May and November."

Fred nodded his head and said, "I am honored!"

The old man walked up and down the line of people. He came back and stopped in front of Ace. He walked slowly around Ace. He spoke two words. Two of the young men parted and motioned Ace to come with them.

TQ again explained, "Ace, you've been selected to be taught the old ways of a warrior. It will take a lot of work and concentration. At the end, if you pass, you will be presented to the tribe for adoption. It is a great honor."

Ace lifted his chin and stepped immediately to the two young men who pointed to the last truck.

They left before the old man made his next choice. First, the old man motioned for TQ to get into line with the others.

TQ hesitated, unsure of the old man's intentions.

Fred commanded, "TQ, get into line next to Manny!"

The old man smiled and nodded as if to tell himself of his wisdom in choosing the patriarch of the clan.

TQ moved quickly to comply.

The old man took the hands of the women and led them out of line. He turned them to face the two young men. He walked behind the women, looking past them toward the men. Then, he moved behind the men and repeated his actions. He spoke.

As the old man pushed Toy toward Manny, TQ interpreted, "The tall black warrior is now Night Bear. This is your woman. She has given you her heart. You must make her life complete. You will give her sons."

TQ smiled and said, "In case you guys didn't get that, he just married you. It will hold up in any court in the country."

Manny tried not to smile as he said, "Tell him I am honored by his wisdom."

Toy spoke quickly and quietly to the old man, "We'll have many strong sons."

TQ cautioned the couple, "The old ways must be kept here. Manny, you will go to the second truck. Toy, you follow just behind. Get in after Manny is settled."

The old man moved in front of Anne and spoke.

TQ smiled grandly and interpreted, "You are married to the tall warrior in spirit already. The Great One speaks of your kind, strong spirit. Warriors are your sons, and they will be your joy in your old age. Your daughter will have the spirit of her father. She will be sought after by many warriors when of age. Be careful not to let her go without wise counsel."

Here the old man turned and looked at Fred. Fred nodded and the old man smiled again at the wisdom of his selection. He spoke and turned abruptly toward the first truck.

TQ hastily explained, "Quick, Fred! Catch up with him, but don't pass him. Get into the front of the first truck just after he does. Anne…."

Anne grinned and said, "I know. I follow behind you and get in after you are settled… my husband!"

It was all TQ could do to keep from letting out a whoop like a brave of old.

The plane taxied and zoomed into the sky almost as soon as the trucks started moving. It flew back over the trucks and dipped a wing once before it disappeared into the high white clouds. An old debt to TQ had just been paid.

The next day, after a long night of riding in the back of the trucks, blankets tucked tightly around them against the cold night air, they were in the mountains of Wyoming. The air was crisp, clean, clear, and invigorating.

43
A New Life

Fred informed the little clan, "I take this mandate seriously. You four will, too. In two days, Toy and Anne will go into the towns of Cody or Meeteetse for supplies. As a group, we are lucky not to have any worries about money since you two had all that money stashed. You keep the amounts to yourselves. Kick in an even split for expenses to get a common enterprise off the ground. It has to be legitimate. I think the best way to hide is to be mixed in with the locals. Be a local citizen, but not in the public eye. No pictures with faces! No places where the public gathers in large crowds or drinks. You two big guys will make every drunk in two counties want to fight to impress some woman."

"Next, I know Eagle Flying married you. I want you both married by a clergy. Hold off on the 'lovey dovey' until we find one."

Manny, looking at Toy, said, "I'll find one Fred."

Toy exclaimed, "Yes he will Fred! I guarantee it!"

Laughing, Manny said, "See, I feel married already!"

A lot happened that Friday:

They bought three miles of lake front property, CASH!

They were incorporated as the Crystal Lake Wilderness Outfitters.

The corporation was to focus on hunting, fishing, cross-country skiing, and trail hiking.

Crystal Lake Wilderness Outfitters, Inc. bought two used late model pickup trucks, five four-wheelers, seven snowmobiles, three large tents for temporary shelter, cots, blankets, lumber, tools, generators, and other materials needed to build cabins.

All the transaction were done through an executive of Crystal Lake Wilderness Outfitters Inc., Fred, dressed in a new suit and tie.

During this time, the companies two big hired hands, TQ and Manny, loaded the materials and supplies on the newly acquired trucks as fast as it was put on the loading dock of the lumber yard.

A local worker pointed at TQ and asked, "You an Indian?"

TQ solemnly replied, "Yep, both Indians."

The local worker looked over at Manny and observed, "He don't look Indian."

TQ more solemnly replied, "Yeah, Blackfoot!"

The local worker looked at TQ with a challenge, "You funning me?"

TQ waved a hand in the air and said, "Don't think I could ever pull anything over on you!"

Manny bent over and started to choke on pent up laughter.

TQ pointed at Manny and said, "Allergies! Can't work a lick without choking up!"

The local worker exclaimed, "What good is he if he can't work!"

TQ pensively stated, "I've wondered about that myself, but he seems to be able to get a lot done. Most around here couldn't keep up with him all day."

Offended, the local worker asked, "Says who?"

TQ says while holding his hands up in front of his chest, "I'm not saying you can't work, OK, but he can go all day it seems. Out works me sometimes, and him with allergies."

Local worker looking at Manny now working about half speed exclaimed, "Why I could work rings around him!"

TQ reached into his pocket and challenged the worker. "I've got twenty dollars says he can load more than anyone else here in the next hour!"

Enthusiastically, the local worker said, "You're on! Out of the way, Blackfoot!"

A second worker asked, "Hey, Mark, what's going on?"

Mark explained to his friend, "This new dude bet me I can't load as much as this Blackfoot. I can beat him with one arm, Pete."

Pete observed, "Looks to me like he's got two speeds... slow and stop! Hey, can I get in on that bet?"

TQ shook his head resignedly and said, "Well, I hate to see you two trying so hard and me knowing you would lose."

Pete had his manhood affronted. He said, "I'll take that bet. Up here, we know how to work. Move over you two!"

The two trucks were loaded in a matter of minutes. Then, they persuaded the two workers to bring their pickups around and load them for forty dollars more and a tank full of gas each.

Mark, the first worker, and Pete, the second worker, proved to be very good workers, if not too bright. TQ made a deal with them to help repair and expand the old existing cabin so our friends could move in quickly. Eventually it would be Fred's home and a place for honored guests. The mountain days and nights are always cold at this time of the year.

In the next twenty-five days, four new things were built:

A large cabin with four bedrooms, new kitchen, family room, meeting room and indoor plumbing.

A pump house to bring water from the lake.

Friendship with the locals.

Two new families. Manny had found the minister he promised!

44
Fast Start

By the time the snow started to melt in late April, the first of many clients arrived, happy to be spending big bucks to live for a short while in the rough beauty of the Wyoming Mountains.

Anne had been teaching Toy to cook and bake. Between them, they had clients asking what was for the next meal before they finished the meal they were eating. The two were always together, like sisters.

TQ and Manny worked hard from just after breakfast, until darkness forced them to quit, every day except Saturday and Sunday. Fred laid down the law. "Only necessary work to make clients comfortable, or emergencies, on Saturday is to be done. No working on Sunday except for an emergency."

The last Sunday in April, Anne spent a lot of time in the bathroom getting ready for the Sunday service Fred held. They only went to a formal church once a month when they went to town to pick up the supplies they ordered over the radio. When she came out of the bedroom, she linked her arm in TQ's and started humming a tune strange to TQ.

TQ said, "You sure are chipper this morning! What's that song you're humming?"

Anne nonchalantly replied, "Braham's Lullaby."

TQ took about three steps from their cabin door and stopped so quickly he had to grab Anne's arm to keep her from falling forward.

TQ asked, "Lullabies are for when you have babies, right?"

Anne smiled broadly and asked her own questions, "What do you think about Mary Elizabeth for a girl and Frederick Paul for a boy?"

TQ threw his hands up in the air and loudly asked Anne, "So, I'm going to be a father, right?"

Anne, laughing now at her husband, said, "Right! So is Manny, but don't spoil it for Toy. I don't know how we'll put up with you two for the next seven or eight months."

TQ said seriously, "Only seven or eight months! We've got to get busy! We both need another bedroom on our cabins. Toys, cribs, highchair, carriage! We have to go shopping!"

Anne grabbed TQ's hand and started for the service, "Today is Sunday and Dad is waiting. We'll shop when we know if it is a son or daughter. Come on big guy!"

TQ was grinning so wide he could hardly keep his mouth closed. He was feeling like his chest would burst!

Anne slid into the chair next to Toy and reached for her hand. They each looked at their respective husbands then smiled at each other.

Manny had his eyes closed and his hands clasped together up by his face. He opened his eyes and looked at TQ with a smile that mirrored the one on TQ's face.

Anne noted, "Well, I see you told Manny!"

Toy squeezed her hand and said, "I had to hold his hand ever since to keep him from floating away like some big balloon."

Fred came in from the kitchen with a cup of coffee. Several guests had joined the group while they waited for Fred. He settled in his chair and said, "Let's pray and thank God for all the good things he gives us."

TQ couldn't stop himself. He fairly yelled, "Thank you Lord for our children!"

To which Manny boomed out, "Aaaaaamen!"

Fred's head snapped up like he was hit on the chin with a hard, right uppercut. He looked back and forth at the smiling foursome for several moments.

Finally, Fred demanded, "Well, spit it out! Don't make me wait all day!"

Manny and TQ started talking fast and very loud! Everyone else broke out in laughter at the two fathers to be until Anne and Toy clamped their hands over each of their husband's respective mouths.

Anne explained, "Dad, Toy and I are pregnant. You're going to be a grandfather twice."

Everyone clapped and cheered. The two new fathers-to-be stood and bowed like they had just been called for an encore at Carnegie Hall.

45
New Trouble Starts

By this time, Spooky and Ricco had recruited four new members, a whole new *Team* However, this *Team* was made up of cutthroats, men without direction or ideals. Ricco had handpicked them all. Spooky had become distant, morose. The more Ricco thought about the situation, the more he blamed TQ for everything. He still didn't know where TQ had disappeared to. Manny, either! He thought Toy was dead. Every day he swore he would kill TQ.

Each of the new members was briefed on picking up information on TQ. They memorized physical characteristics, habits, movements, speech patterns, likes, and dislikes.

Their *Team* took on jobs for anyone able to pay the price. They even double-crossed one client to another for extra money. When they were done, there was no one left to protest. It was a massacre blamed on a radical religious group. It actually had its roots in greed and a grab for power.

This went on for over three years. Then, an old client looked them up for a new job. The client mentioned off-handedly he had seen TQ in Wyoming. TQ was running a wilderness outfitter and guide operation. No, he hadn't spoken to TQ, but he was sure there were not two men like TQ. The evil smile on Ricco's face was mirrored by the hate in his eyes. Spooky involuntarily took two steps back, stopped by the edge of a table.

46
Back to Crystal Lake

On July 2nd of the second year, Fred received an invitation from Eagle Flying to a ceremony for the whole group. It was a ceremony which normally excluded all but Native Americans. This new clan was to be an exception. Cunning Wolf, as Ace was now known, was to be adopted into the tribe and given warrior status! Cunning Wolf had expressly asked to have the big black warrior present. The ceremony was to take place the next full moon.

Manny was surprised by the changes in Ace, Cunning Wolf, when he first laid eyes on him. He had gained weight. His shoulders were wider and his chest was deeper. He had a very little waist and was bronzed all over by the sun. The potential for leadership which had been apparent in his knowledge and character had been welded to the physical make up of a Greek god. To verify this, one only had to look at the large group of unmarried young ladies giggling and batting eyelashes in his direction. The ceremony was secret; the old ways were observed. We'll leave it at that.

Business was booming. Money flowed in from people who wanted to escape their mundane lives and live on the edge of the wildness, testing their spirits and bodies for a week or two. Stables and horses had been added the second year. A few pack mules rounded out the experience for the hardier souls. God was smiling on them all.

47
The Good Life

Time and success had brought the hope the old life was past – was indeed over. The corporation now had eleven full-time employees and fourteen more who worked only during the summer months. Time was passing, pleasantly.

Manny had taken to the woods and tracking almost as fast as TQ could teach him. He now guided his share of the hunting parties.

That was great with TQ. He still felt uncomfortable when he was very far from his family. TQ felt he was leaving them vulnerable. He thought the others considered it over, that they were safe. In his heart, TQ knew it was not the case. Ricco and Spooky would never stop until either they or TQ were dead. It was a sickness TQ knew Ricco had. TQ had seen the changes in Spooky before he left, also. The two were deceived. They would validate their own deceptions by feeding off each other. If they could only find what mattered most, Jesus!

TQ counted his blessings! Anne, Fred, two sons (Frederic Paul and Quincy Manfred,) Paul and Katie, Manny and Toy with their two children (Rebekah Marie and Manfred Turner,) Cunning Wolf (Ace) and Blue Flower (Alice,) his wife, of one year were expecting their first child in a couple of months. TQ wanted to keep them all safe. He prayed for it every night.

TQ and Manny had added onto their cabins twice since they were initially built. They weren't cabins anymore. They were large, comfortable homes.

It was Manny who nicknamed Frederic Paul as FP when he was only three days old. It stuck much to Anne's initial dismay and a smile from TQ. FP was constantly under his father's feet or riding on TQ's shoulders. Both Anne and TQ would smile as FP tried to do the things his father was doing. At three years and eleven months, FP couldn't read much, but he could tell you the names of twenty-eight animals or birds from their tracks and feces.

Anne would be prepared to scold both of them when they would come in from the forest late for supper, until FP would reach up to kiss her face and say, "Tradition Mama." How could anyone be upset?

She would laugh a little and wait to receive a kiss from TQ who would very solemnly say, "Traditions must be maintained." Then, TQ would give her a wink and a smile.

Anne would throw up her hands in mock exasperation and say, "Lord, what am I going to do with these men." Sometimes little Quincy would raise his hands and laugh, too.

Anne thought everything was wonderful, it just couldn't get any better. It was good she couldn't see the future.

FP had been born strong, hollering, and with a thick head of dark hair, just like TQ. From the start, he wanted things his own way. Even his mother had a hard time getting him to quiet down.

TQ would enter the scene, lift the baby high in the air, and say, "FP, you have to give your Mama and God some peace."

TQ would cradle the baby in his big arms and chant old Navajo songs. In less than two minutes, FP was either smiling or asleep. Even now, FP would only go directly to bed, without a fuss, at just one word from TQ.

Quincy was a lot like his older brother, but he preferred the soft feel of his mother's arms and her voice singing to him. He was a contrast with skin of a copper hue, piercing green eyes, and auburn hair. His eyes seemed to look through you into your heart.

It was supper time when TQ, Manny, and FP returned from town in Manny's dark blue Super Duty Ford pickup. FP would be four on January 11th, just five days from now.

While in town, Uncle Manny had taken FP for hot chocolate while TQ shopped for birthday presents which he stashed under the tarp in the back of Manny's truck. It was Manny, looking out the little shop window, who noticed the two unfamiliar men leaning on a SUV. They turned slightly, conversing closely, sneaking covert looks at TQ when he came out of a store with his arms full of presents for FP. Manny almost dismissed them when they got into the SUV as if to drive away. After all, lots of people would make comments and look at TQ two or three times. There weren't many people like TQ anywhere and no others like him in this vicinity. Manny and TQ would often laugh at the looks and the comments the two men drew as they rode back from town. Yes, Manny almost dismissed them, until one got out and sat in a chair in front of the Café where he could watch the whole street.

Manny didn't want to upset FP. He would talk to TQ back at the lake. They would make plans there. Fred was there. Paul and Katie were due in sometime tonight. Ace and his family would be here tomorrow. BJ couldn't make it until the 11th, FP's birthday. FP's birthday had become the day the whole group got together, like a family reunion.

Manny was ready! If anything, he was keener under TQ's training. He never realized how little he knew until he started going into the forest with TQ. The man was amazing! He was an amazing friend, closer than a brother, as the Bible said.

After the presents were stashed out of site, the three went shopping for the items and groceries on the lists Toy and Anne had prepared.

Manny was unprepared for the answer when he asked TQ, "Hey, TQ, what's this thing?"

TQ came back with, "What thing?"

Manny replied, "EPT! What's an EPT?"

TQ teased Manny, "Why you old dog! No kidding?"

Manny was totally baffled and said, "No kidding, what? Come on, TQ!"

TQ changed directions in the middle of the street. Then he said, "Next stop is the Pharmacy. Manny, my friend, Toy wants a pregnancy test!"

Right then and there, Manny forgot all about the shopping list and the two strange men! He only wanted to hurry back and use the new test. He had TQ drive so he could read the directions. He read them so many times on the way back home, he had them memorized.

48
Treachery

When they reached the lake, Manny hurriedly helped TQ unload the items on Anne's grocery list and promised to return later with the gifts stashed under the tarp. He was focused on getting the EPT test home to Toy.

Anne declared, "Supper's ready! Before you take off those boots and coats, get some wood for the fires. It's going to be a cold one!"

TQ broke the news to Anne, "Hey, Toy had Manny pick up an EPT!"

Anne wonderingly shook her head and said, "Men, you're so slow about these things! She told me she thought she was pregnant almost two weeks ago."

Outside it was dark, pitch black, no moon. TQ loaded a log carrier to cut down on his trips. The wood boxes needed to be full this cold night. FP carried three small pieces of kindling. They had LP gas to cook on and oil heat for a backup. Primarily, they used wood for everything. Cutting wood was good exercise and it was plentiful. Fred arrived to help with the last load of firewood. Four times a week he had supper with TQ's family. Three times a week he made sure he spent time with Manny's family over a supper meal.

When the supper dishes were cleared away, Fred remarked, "My FP, how big you are for five years old!"

FP exclaimed, "I'm not five, Poppa! I'm gonna be four!" Then he jumped up on a chair and said, "I'm as big as Daddy!"

As TQ scooped him up with one arm and tickled him with the other, the kitchen window shattered and TQ felt the shock of a bullet go through his right shoulder. By instinct, he hit the floor and covered FP with his body! He hollered for Fred to grab the rifle by the door and cover them as the lights were shut off by Anne. TQ rose cradling his son when the lights went out.

It was totally silent for about 10 seconds. The sound of a scream from outside was followed immediately by a second scream in the cozy kitchen. The second scream was Anne, the mother of FP. That scream brought TQ to realize she was looking at the bloody inert form of their son in the flickering light from the fireplace.

Just five days short of his fourth birthday, the toddler lay in his father's arms with blood covering his little body. His father held him close and his mother sobbed and frantically reached for him. Turner Quincy Freeman (TQ), US Army Special Forces, retired early by a death fabricated by a government agency, a death more permanent than real, stood holding his son. Silent tears fell from his cheeks to mingle with the blood from his shoulder wound which flowed down to mix with the blood of his son. The wound was from an assassin's rifle.

TQ barely heard Manny yell, "It's Manny. I'm coming in!"

In one glance Manny took in the whole situation.

Manny exclaimed in agonizing tones, "Oh, no! God, no! It's my fault! How is he? TQ, snap out of it, man! We have to check his vitals! Give him to me! Anne, run over and get Toy! Fred, call the Air Ambulance! He's still alive. It looks like the bullet passed through you and creased him on the left side of the head. Sit down, TQ. Fred, stop his shoulder bleeding. I'll clean FP up so I can make sure of the wound. You ready to hear me out, TQ?"

TQ looked at Manny and a chill ran the whole length of Manny's body. Never had he seen a look like that on any human being! He could only imagine it was the same look a mother grizzly would get if her cubs are threatened.

Anne and Toy burst through the door. Anne reached again for her son. Manny gently placed the unconscious boy in his mother's arms.

Fred came back from the radio room and said, "I called the Air Ambulance! They should be here in less than ten minutes."

Manny directed his wife, "Toy, get ice on his head. Put it on his whole head, not just the wound. We have to keep his brain from swelling."

Fred demanded, "Who was it? Where is the rat?"

Manny pointed toward a knoll and said, "Out there! I'm afraid he is no longer able to say anything. TQ, forgive me man! I picked up on two guys in town. I was going to let you know when we got back here, private. I forgot all about them when the EPT came up. Sorry, man!"

TQ reached out with his good left hand, "Brothers!" That was all he said.

Manny took the hand. They held that way for a full minute. FP hadn't moved.

Manny filled them in. "TQ, Fred, there were at least two. They had a dark green SUV. It was a Chevy Blazer I think. Probably a rental! They took pains so you wouldn't notice them. One left in the SUV. The other watched. I'm going out now to see if I can back track this guy."

TQ announced, "I'm coming, too!"

Fred ordered, "No! You're hurt and you're needed here. I'll go with Manny. I've picked up a few things around you guys in the last couple of years. Besides, I can hold that big flashlight for Manny."

Manny reassured TQ by saying, "When we get all the info we can here, we'll need you strong and thinking straight to help us run these guys down. We have to or there won't be any future for our families."

TQ looked at the still form of his eldest son in his mother's arms. He took in the rest of the crying children clinging to their distraught mothers.

TQ knew what he had to do. He explained it to his father-in-law this way, "Fred, I know what God's word says about forgiveness and revenge. Forgiveness is only good to the doers of foulness, if this they stop, and if they can accept the forgiveness. We will forgive them for this so there is nothing between us and what God wants. He also says in his word that crimes here are to be punished here. He will take care of judging the spirit in due time. Anne told me that God made me a soldier, His soldier. She wisely told me to accept it and fight only when necessary; fight for the right things. This is the right thing! This is necessary! I will be God's soldier."

49

Awakening

Eyelids fluttered slowly, weakly, against the bright rays of sunlight streaming through the dirty window, invading the little room reeking with the smell of old bloodied bandages lying in the corner next to the closed, dirty, solitary window. Spooky Harris should have been dead in the bush of Africa, three months earlier.

He was only semi-conscious of the slight pain and stiffness in his left leg and right hand from the last job in Africa. The extreme weakness he felt was weighing him down, he barely had the strength to lift a limb. It cost his *Team* two men, mercenaries, and wounds which almost cost Spooky his life. The wound to his left thigh was bad, almost causing him to bleed out. Ricco stood over him, just staring, some form of jubilant expectation shining from his eyes. Carlton Trostle, a new recruit, fresh out of the Army and battlefields, slowed the bleeding and carried him to the extraction site.

Spooky still couldn't get the look on Ricco's face out of his mind. During lucid moments, Spooky had listened to Ricco whispering to the four remaining team members and observing the openly sinister side glances of members of the team whenever they poked their heads in the room to see if he was still alive. Only Trostle seemed almost friendly. Spooky suddenly realized he owed his life to this Trostle fellow. Carlton Trostle! It seemed like a normal given name. He knew it wasn't and Spooky wondered who he owed his life to.

He didn't have a prayer of thanks! That word had never been in his life, not until twelve-year old Rosita came into his life. Spooky never had a wife, live-in girlfriend, or kids… never wanted any. What changed? Why was it suddenly so important to a man who hadn't been able to get out of bed, bathe or go to the bathroom by himself for three months he see Rosita and her mother, Esmerelda.

Just a few moments ago, Trostle entered the room where Spooky lay on a filthy mattress, no sheet, no pillow. Trostle, sporting a new mustache, exclaimed a little too loudly if Spooky wanted to get his strength back he needed to get out in the sun and move around. Good and correct advice but something was up. It was a little too loud like a subtle warning. It had the feel of urgency and some fear. Yeah, Spooky reminded himself he never feared anything, not until this mess started with the Ghost in what seemed a lifetime ago.

Trostle had a couple of sandwiches and a bottle of water stuffed in his jacket pockets. Spooky offered him a hand, which Trostle grabbed with his left hand and pulled Spooky to his feet; handing him the homemade crutches he had in his right hand when Spooky fell weakly into Trostle's chest. It was then the jacket opened and Spooky viewed four guns and a knife stuck in the waist band of his cargo pants. Catching Spooky's glance, Trostle merely whispered, "Outside." Spooky's voice sounded a little shrill to himself when he responded it would be good to sit in the sunshine. Trostle and Spooky navigated their way past the others and out the door where Trostle steered him abruptly left toward some boulders on the cliff's edge with a view of the Pacific Ocean and a path to the village on the beach.

On a boulder facing the little house behind Spooky, Trostle talked of the weather and war stories as he slowly and carefully, always observing the door and one visible window of the house, placed the sandwiches, water, two automatic weapons, and ammunition on the ground between Spooky and himself, always sitting erect in case they were being observed.

Spooky's normally keen mind was struggling to work past the physical pain and weakness to put together the immediate actions of Trostle, the others on the team, and Ricco's hostile looks into a solid evaluation of his current situation, whether he was about to live or die.

What could it mean? Suddenly he wasn't needed, he was a liability. It couldn't be the money they had accumulated. Spooky had always made sure his cut of the money they received went straight to places no one but he could touch. There was nothing else. Or was there!

Wait! There was one thing; only one thing… they had located TQ! All of a sudden, it was vividly clear. Spooky had changed his mind about hunting down TQ. Time between events and the prior year he spent with the Rose and Esmeralda had mellowed his hard heart. He was finally free, but didn't have the guts to tell Ricco he was out. He admitted he was more afraid of Ricco than he was of TQ. What had Manny called Ricco? Oh yeah, a loose cannon!

TQ and all he loved were in deadly imminent danger. In a panic, Spooky realized he must escape his *Team* if he was to survive, change his life and warn TQ. Suddenly he saw he was now in the position TQ was in years ago. He had to get Rosita and her mother to safety. Her mother, Esmerelda, pretty on the outside and truly beautiful on the inside with a quiet spirit he still didn't understand. Spooky wanted that peaceful spirit, he wanted her. He had to go now! Spooky would take Esmerelda and Rosita to a better place, a better life if they would have him.

Could he trust Trostle to help him? He turned to find Trostle was no longer with him, he was alone. He had to move, even in his weakened state. Slowly the panic on his face was replaced by a firm resolve and a firmness around the eyes that spoke of the extreme lengths he would use to succeed in this unfamiliar situation life threw at him. Unconsciously, Spooky glanced toward the sky for help, still unable to voice a prayer.

Had Spooky glanced over his right shoulder, at that moment in time, he would have felt a tingle of fear at the flash of sunlight off the barrel of the high-powered sniper rifle aimed between his shoulder blades, centered on his spine.

The man holding the rifle is of no importance. He was another mercenary replacing one killed recently in Africa. No, the power of life and death was behind the cold, cruel, flickering eyes of Ricco. It made him feel a little like a god to tell the man with his finger on the trigger to let Spooky live for now. Ricco's smile reflected how good he felt holding the power of life and death. He was in charge, as it always should have been. He had a plan of action. He would show them all that only he, Ricco, was in charge. He told himself he was like a god, no, he was a god!

50
Answers Wait for Morning

FP's parents spent the long, cold night, alternating between his bedside and the tiny chapel of the hospital. All night they prayed and listened to the patient alarms and two Code Blue calls over the PA system, afraid the code calls might be for their son.

As morning broke over the mountain and the bright sun rays leaped into the room to shine on FP, highlighting his innocent face against the stark white sheets and bandages around his head, he blinked quickly and tried to turn away from the sun's intrusion. TQ remained watching from the doorway, his big heart melting, feeling insignificant and small, as he watched his wife sleeping while she held tight to FP's little hand, and FP stirring when a team of doctors said he would probably be in a coma for weeks or months. Right then and there, in that doorway, TQ quoted Lamentations 3:22-23, "Through the Lord's mercies we are not consumed, because His compassions fail not. They are new every morning: Great is your faithfulness."

With tears streaming down his face, he fell on his knees by the bed and hugged both his wife and child with trembling arms and, in a loud baritone voice, began singing *Amazing Grace* which drew nurses and doctors with bowed heads into the doorway of the room. Through the crowded doorway pushed a small nurse with long black braids. She smiled, like she had known this was the way it would resolve, and slowly faded back into the crowd and disappeared. When asked, no one could say they had even seen her or knew who she was.

51
Preparing for War

A large group of family, friends, and neighbors were gathered in the great room of the log cabin that was home to TQ's family during the good times and now, in this tragedy. Loud and silent prayers had been ascending to the throne of God all night. The children were sleeping at Manny and Toy's house, surrounded by armed men, comforted and watched over by three grandmotherly women of God from their church family in town. The difference between the two houses went way beyond the locations. The peace and comfort at Manny's house was in direct contrast to the harsh conversation of tactics and strategy required for ferreting out an enemy of unknown location, characteristics, quantity, experience, and expertise.

The main question was, "What was the enemy doing to prepare?

Strategy is basically determining what assets would be needed to defeat the foe, where and when to place them. Tactics are the timing, speed, and movement of those assets to get the mission completed with as little casualties on your side as possible.

TQ slowly let his gaze sweep the room packed with people of good hearts and great intentions. They weren't trained and there was no time. A plan was forming, a plan which put him and Manny in extreme danger and employed a much smaller force of men with centuries of experience and training infused into their very souls, warriors every one.

Manny had just come to the same conclusion, they could not put their families and friends in certain danger when he caught the kitchen door go slightly, softly ajar. Suddenly he smiled hugely. He remembered his little 'brother,' Ace, and four men from his new Navaho family had disappeared into the dark cold night through that very door about forty minutes ago. Still, he put his hand on the Glock in his pocket and turned slightly toward the door as he directed the attention of both federal agents in that direction with a nod of his head.

52
Unexpected Ally

Quietly, Ace entered but didn't fully close the door. When he turned and went back out that same door, Manny, Paul and Katie were only a second behind him. Surprise! Another large man with the breeding of a warrior emanating from his posture, was backed against a tree with his hands behind his head and four lever-action carbines leveled at him from six feet away. He was neatly caught for sure!

The man looked directly at Manny and asked, "Does everyone here move as quietly as these guys?"

Manny suggested just as directly, without smiling, "You're lucky to be alive. How long depends on what you have to say and if we believe you. No one would ever find a trace of you if you lie to us."

"I answer to Jake. For about six months I went by Carlton Trostle. I'll only speak to a man I never met, TQ. I can wait in the cold. I'm used to it. It's silly for me to sit here with my hands in the air. If you want to shoot me for dropping my hands, then go ahead. "

Katie volunteered, "I'll get TQ." When she walks into the room packed with well-meaning family and friends, TQ quickly spots her, nods his head and finished telling everyone his plan.

"Too many people mean that a lot will get hurt or worse. Teams are not large for a number of reasons. The best team with the most chance of success is smaller, experienced, qualified people with the right frame of mind. We will pick the team we need to fit the mission and ask the rest of you to go home and pray continually for us while we are gone. Excuse me a minute."

TQ stopped on the second step and looked intently at the man seated in the snow against the tree. "I don't know your name, but I've seen your picture a number of times. How's your Father these days?"

As Jake rose and walked toward TQ, the business ends of the rifles unwaveringly followed his every step. When he stopped in front of TQ and started to speak, he was smiling broadly. "It's nice to have friends. You have a lot of them. Dad talks of you often. Don't see him much, but we talk a couple of times a week. We were looking for you quite a while and you sure didn't make it easy. Dad likes to pay his debts and sends his thanks for that Black Sea thing."

TQ's broad shoulders moved in a slight shrug, "Glad to help. How did you find us?"

Jake glanced at the unwavering rifle muzzles and continued, "I didn't. Dad said to hook-up with your enemies and let them do the work. They have a more extensive information network than we have. I just arrived from the West Coast of Mexico. You need to know Ricco has taken over and is nuts over finding you. I mean, totally off the deep end. Spooky let Ricco know he is out. It seems he met a pretty Mexican woman with a little girl. He realized that he has become you, in a manner of speaking. He is risking his life right now and I'm not sure he is aware of it. Did my best to give him a head start out of there, but I don't think he will leave the ladies there by themselves. I'm a little nervous with those rifles still pointed at me."

Manny waved a big hand and the rifles suddenly pointed at the ground.

TQ introduced the son of an old friend, "Meet Jake Hadzhier, the only son of an old enemy and one of my dearest friends, Bizer Hadzhier from Bulgaria." TQ turns and opened the door, the whole group followed him into the warm room for coffee and time to get acquainted with the new recruit.

53
Selected to Fight

As TQ was pouring cups of hot coffee from the big urn for all the half-frozen group recently in out of the cold and snow, Jake whispered in TQ's ear. "Dad is waiting fifteen miles off the coast of San Diego for your signal. He will get all of us to the right place on the Pacific coast of Mexico, go back out to sea, and when signaled, pick everyone up after it is over. Burial at sea would be proper and no mess for any of the other team who don't survive. Weapons and other necessary things are already on board his ship. We don't have to worry about transporting articles that would be illegal to take across state lines."

TQ turned to hand Jake his coffee and gave an almost imperceptible nod in the direction of the master bedroom. He spoke out-loud, "Looks like I'll be pouring coffee for another ten minutes. Check on Manny's coffee first. Then check on Fred, Paul, Ace, and the Chief. We should all have full cups, coffee that will last at least twenty minutes." This new information solidified the plan of action TQ had been mulling over for about four hours to those he just mentioned.

Ten minutes later, TQ entered his master bedroom with a steaming cup of black coffee to join his war council. When TQ furnished the latest strategic information, five battle tested veterans nodded in unison and breathed a collective sigh of relief. That immense weight, forming a viable plan, now off their shoulders, was reflected in the smoothing of the deep lines which had formed on all of their faces. Waiting is over.

TQ's cup moved a couple of inches in Manny's direction, "Manny is in charge of times to leave here, to meet the boat, food, and papers needed for all participants. Jake will coordinate with him on the weapons we want against what is available now and what is needed to do when it is over, the clean-up. Paul and the Chief will select fifteen of the best trained and reliable Navaho men available, brief them on what's coming up. No one will be forced to go. Most have families of their own. Ace will be in charge of half of the braves and Paul the other half. Fred and the Chief will remain here, in charge of the remaining force that they select for security against an unexpected attack. Don't forget our women! I'm sure they will remind you of their experience and expertise. Keep them all here. Send all the rest of our family and friends home. Have enough supplies for a month and ammunition to fight WWIII. Questions! None! We will each get a turn to pray. Then we'll get to it. We are leaving here bright and early, tomorrow morning, by 0800."

54
Another Plan

At the same moment, above that quiet Mexican village, Ricco was dictating orders to eleven mercenaries that comprised his current team.

"We found TQ. We have them all. Brice reported Teo shot and killed TQ, but Manny killed Teo. Brice dumped Teo where he might never be found. We don't want the Feds and locals in our way. I want to kill them all; all of their families, pets, everything! I'm going to cut Manny into little pieces for the scavengers to feed on. There are seven more guys coming by the day after tomorrow. I'll spell out the plan two days after that, after we get familiar with each other, our jobs, weapons and such. We head North six days from now. No one touches Spooky. That traitor I want all to myself when we get back here! In short, we will truck to the border and use the tunnels for smuggling dope into the States as our way in. There will be motor homes on the other side waiting to transport us to Wyoming. Might as well ride in comfort for those three days. In Wyoming, they will still be reeling at TQ's death. The Ghost will haunt me no more! It will be easy pickings for sure. Bonus money for all who return!"

Ricco had flawed intelligence reports. That is a bane for all who fight any war. What will happen is hard to guess.

55
Anxiety and Peace

Some of the greatest stories of love have come out of war, fear for a future without the one we love, a feeling of need to have that love now before it is too late. That would have been the sum of Spooky's feelings as he limped closer to the little house of Esmerelda and the child Rosita only a hundred yards away. Like an apparition, Esmerelda appeared, running as fast as she could to take him in her arms. Rosita arrived a second later and the only two ladies who Spooky/Ken ever allowed in his life took him home. He kept repeating in his mind, "Home, home, home."

Esmerelda had been speaking so rapidly in Spanish all the way to the house, Spooky couldn't understand what she was trying to say. When they finally lay him on the clean sheets of the bed he said in Spanish, "You will have to tell me all over again, slowly. I only understood about half of what you said."

Esmerelda knelt by the bed, took his hand in both of hers, looked searchingly into his face and began again. "Spooky, my love, we, have been so worried about you for months. We have been praying for you to not do this thing anymore. Please stay here with me. We don't need much money, just God and each other."

It took Spooky several seconds to realize he was no longer frightened or worried. A huge smile filled his mouth, eyes, his whole countenance. "Ken, it's Ken, not Spooky anymore. Yes, I will stay here with you, my love, always. First, we will be married in the church and then we will be a family. I feel like God has made me new."

Esmerelda, with a quiet voice, and loving smile, returned, "He has my love... my husband. Little Rosita put her arms around Ken's neck and whispered in his ear, "Papa."

Ken knew it was not over. He knew he was in no shape to go to Wyoming to help TQ. He knew he had to stay right here. Last, he knew this was in God's hands, God would protect them. Peace flooded his soul and body. He drifted off to sleep with Rosita hugging his neck and Esmerelda holding his hand.

56
Hidden in The Mist

Everything went right on schedule for moving TQ's team of recruits from Wyoming to a little marina just north of San Diego, loaded onto charter fishing boats, and meeting Captain Biser fifteen miles out on a misty sea, visibility was a few hundred feet. That was thirty-eight hours ago. Within four hours they would be picked up by local fishermen in the heavy warm mist of what was to become a sunny day in Western Mexico. Manny had been going over scenario after possible scenario, plan after plan, so all of their team could be successful and return to their families alive and well. Everyone knew, but didn't voice, the possibility of no casualties was zero.

When they left, a few of the younger women had shed some tears, but all had blessed them and began praying for their safety and success. Toy kept massaging the butt of her Glock automatic, all the while comforting first one, then another of the women as their men were whisked away in trucks. She did not voice a single syllable of fear, though in her heart there was a cold foreboding in the mist which chilled the body and soul. She lifted another prayer.

The voyage was tense to the Mexican coastline, but now, a bright red flare cut through the Pacific Ocean mist and signaled the arrival of the Mexican fisherman. Ace suddenly was in front of Manny voicing nothing for about fifteen seconds; studying Manny's face as if to etch it into his memory as into a fine marble monument. He reached out and took Manny's hand in a firm grip and said, "I don't know if I'll make it home but I wouldn't have it any other way, big brother." Manny grabbed Ace in a hug which seemed to take too long then held him at arms-length and said, "Go with God little brother." They melted into the mist to their respective posts, committed to fight for the right, no matter the consequences; maybe the last look, the last embrace for a lifetime memory. Manny reflected Ace truly had the warrior-spirit and honored him in his heart. He looked up, put his right hand over his heart for a second, and raised it as a salute to his Savior.

Making only whispering sounds, the fishing boats were soon headed to an uncertain destiny and the village docks shrouded by the early morning mist.

57
Forewarned, Forearmed

Every big city, every little town or village in any country, has people ready to sell out to an enemy, to evil, from the greed in the human heart. This quiet fishing village was no exception! Miguel, a trusted first cousin of Esmerelda, was privy to all sorts of family business, is trusted but not trustworthy. He knew the hard faced, crazy gringo on the hill above the village had lots of money. Miguel wanted a truck, a nice truck. The crazy gringo with the evil in his eyes was sure to want the information. He would pay greatly to know boat loads of armed men were coming very soon to surround them and kill them. Miguel had to hurry. The morning mist was giving way to another day of bright sunshine even as he ran up the path to the top of the hill.

"Another step and you die!" A voice said in perfect Spanish, which suddenly made Miguel stumble as he tried to instantly stop.

Miguel, out of breath from the unfamiliar exertion, blurted, "A large group of armed Americanos is right now landing at the fishing docks to kill you and the Jeffe, your boss.

Another hard-faced man grabbed Miguel by the back of the neck and propelled him toward the house at a speed Miguel had never thought he could achieve. Suddenly, the door opened and Miguel was thrust through the door where he tripped and fell sprawling on the dirty wood floor. As Miguel started to rise, the weight of a huge man attached to a large booted foot pressed hard between Miguel's shoulders, effectively pinning him to the floor. Miguel had a sinking feeling he might not get paid as much for his information as he first thought.

The guard told Ricco what the Mexican man told him. Ricco smiled evilly and growled, "The rats are coming to us! Get everyone out to their battle positions. We don't know who they are, but it is certain Manny will be leading them, with TQ dead. I want him alive, you understand. I am going to cut him so many times that he will be begging me to kill him."

Ricco started to chuckle quietly as the men scramble to their positions, loaded with extra weapons and ammunition. Out loud he laughed now, high pitched and eerie, like the sound from a character in low budget horror film. Miguel unconsciously curled into a fetal position and prayed God will get him safely home. He had a little money, enough, and his rusty truck would last another five years with a little fixing. Ricco retrieved his own weapons and ammunition and strode out to battle like a true king; a king or a fool. Which will it be?

Miguel, still in the fetal position on the dirty wood floor, suddenly realized he was alone. His fear now magnified that the hard-faced man would comeback rushes adrenaline through his body lending him strength and speed he could not believe as he raced down the path to the village to the safety of his cousin's house. Esmerelda' new husband is still weak but has lots of guns and skill to protect Miguel. He was not concerned about his cousin or her daughter, Rosita.

With no courtesy, and fear still driving all his emotions, Miguel burst through the door to the little adobe house to be brought up very short by two guns pointed at his head by Mr. Ken. Miguel, fed by this new fear, could not stop talking, stumbling over his words, rocking from side to side and swinging his dirty fisted hands back and forth in front of his face like a scared child.

Ken told Miguel to go home and pray for his soul, his treacherous soul.

58
Moving Out

As Manny and his portion of their team advanced directly toward the house on the hill, he was acutely aware the mist was rapidly dissipating under the bright sun; they would be totally visible, their element of surprise gone in less than five minutes. He gave new orders in a soft but harsh whisper. "We will be completely in the open shortly. Find cover and only move forward to another cover when you can."

Ace and Jake had the other two units; Ace moving through the village, house to house, and Jake farther up the hill in the brush and trees. Manny made a short prayer for both of the units, especially Ace's group. They would be covered by Ricco's men from above and had to advance up hill in a much more open scenario.

The last time Manny had eyes on TQ was for a split second as the fishing boat bumped into the dock. TQ gave Manny a thumbs-up and a smile, then disappeared along the beach and into the mist. Where was he, what was he going to do? Go right for the head of the snake? He would be going to find Ricco. He knew that the others, mercenaries all, give up and go when they realized they were no longer drawing wages. They did not know any of their adversaries and had no axe to grind and no loyalty to Ricco except for the money. Manny had a bad feeling!

He never had a bad feeling before in his life. The feeling of foreboding and helplessness was like a heavy weight, crippling his mind and sapping his physical strength. Manny felt like they had already lost the battle. He thought he was hearing someone whisper, "Save yourself. Turn around and go back to your wife and children. You don't really know these people. You owe them nothing."

Then it happened. His toe caught on a rock or tuft of grass, something that threw him forward and down on his hands and knees. Manny didn't feel like he could muster the strength to rise to his feet. Suddenly, Manny realized he was right where he was supposed to be, humble before an almighty God, the Creator, his strength and shield. He prayed, "I am weak, you are strong. I can't do anything without your help. Greater are you in me than anything or anyone out there against me. I'll do your will. You make it happen. Thanks God. In Jesus' name, Amen."

Suddenly, Manny was aware the mist was gone and he had fallen behind a large boulder. Manny smiled, looked toward heaven, and said, "Sorry I doubted you Father. Give me the right decisions. Save us." The angry whine of a bullet sounded as it clipped the boulder near his head.

Manny took in the scene of a true battle field. Men from both sides were trying to find a target, some just shooting at whatever brush or rocks they thought might be hiding an enemy combatant. From the right, close to the sea and out of a normal rifle shot, Manny saw three men dragging a limp form. They had TQ! How?

59

Unexpected Pain

The mist was lifting and TQ had to get behind the enemy. He picked up the pace, running as fast as he could when it happened. Pain, terrible pain, and uncontrollable thrashing of his body. As the thrashing and some pain was subsiding, TQ realized he has been hit by a Taser, actually two Tasers, expertly applied by two members of Ricco's mercenary team. He couldn't move; there was no way to fight or save himself. He should have known Ricco would have thought of this. TQ had trained the old *Team* for just such a situation. One of the men rolled him over on his face in the sand and applied a heavy tie-wrap around his wrists. Two men grabbed him by the arms and roughly dragged him by the arms up the hill to a fate that certainly included more pain and death. All he could do was try to regain his breathing and pray, knowing God was listening.

What none of them noticed was a little girl, frightfully peaking around the corner of the little adobe house the three mercenaries had been hiding behind when they tasered TQ. As the men struggled with TQ's limp body up the path toward Ricco, the little girl slipped into the back door of her house to tell Papa Ken what she had just seen behind their house.

Papa Ken was suddenly Spooky once again. He tucked the two automatics into his waist band, stuffed loaded clips into his pockets, and grabbed the heavy sniper rifle case from the corner, hidden behind the coats hanging on a rack. From this custom case, he extracted a sniper weapon, hand-made and tooled to a perfection only the best of the best could appreciate. He ran his hand up and down the barrel and patted the receiver almost lovingly. As he turned to the door, he said to the rifle, "Well old girl, shoot true, one more time."

Esmerelda said, "Ken, no, please no!"

Ken's face pleaded for understanding as he voiced, "If Ricco wins, we are all dead and we will die horribly. I go for the right reasons, you and Rosita. Pray!" He backed out the door, paused to blow her a quick kiss, turned, and disappeared around the corner of the small church down the street. The mist was gone, but nothing was clear in Esmerelda's mind or heart.

60
Horrible Frightening Noise

The grade of the sandy uphill path was taxing all the strength Ken, Spooky, had left in his still frail body. By the time he reached the relatively level surface at the top, Ken was exhausted and had to lean on the nearest palm tree that would hold him up. The rifle felt so heavy. Maybe Esmerelda was right. Maybe it was no longer his fight. Just as quickly, all he knew about Ricco flooded his brain; the hate, cruelty, and the way he enjoyed hurting others made Ken physically shiver in the warm morning sun.

Spooky struggled dragging the heavy rifle by the sling toward the rocky knoll which overlooked the whole battlefield over five-hundred yards away. He could see the three men hitting and kicking TQ as they forced the weakened man to a certain horrible fate at Ricco's hand. Spooky's resolve solidified; he would end this evil now. He turned back to the path and the nest of rocks where he would shoot from and immediately whipped his attention back toward the area where the continuous volley of gun fire had been a second before.

Jake was Bulgarian by birth. His great grandfather, Ian Trostle, was Scottish and a soldier's soldier, a decorated member of the world renowned and fiercely fighting *Black Watch*. An expert in any weapon of the day, he had another skill that had been passed down through the generations. Bagpipes! Jake was dressed in the kilt of his family colors, hat cocked rakishly, bag filled with air, and stepped proudly out of the brush and trees, oblivious of the danger, and let the shrill tones of ancient war songs scream across the field of battle. All shooting abruptly stopped at the horribly frightening sounds coming from the ancient apparition striding from the trees.

Suddenly, a burly mercenary near the center of the field of battle, stood up, slung his weapon over his shoulder, snapped to attention, and with a smart salute and a proud step marched toward Jake. Then, another on the right and a third near the back broke position and walked after the first man. Their Scottish heritage, and the bond of fighting men everywhere, overcame the here and now. They marched back in time to join with Jake in the celebration of life or death for a cause greater than themselves. No one raised a hand against them. Those not moving toward Jake were melting away through the brush and trees to somewhere else, anywhere else. The battle was suddenly over as TQ was forced to kneel at Ricco's feet.

61
Imminent End

Ricco was overjoyed. His plan of battle was gone, his team deserting, but his evil smile reflected the evil light in his eyes. He would show all of them. He would kill TQ!

Even the best, the strongest, man can be beaten down, body weakened, arms and legs like lead. Forced to his knees, yet true to his heritage, TQ focused his eyes on Ricco, attentive to every movement, every evil word and Ricco's gloating smile.

TQ, knowing and accepting his fate, turned his remaining moments to praying for his family. They may never know his end, but he was sure God would honor the prayers of His soldier dying in the battle against evil. God would protect TQ's family and grow his children into arrows for God's army. Ricco's maniacal laughter brought TQ back to the certain reality of his imminent physical death.

Ricco was boasting about what he would do to the women and then the children. He was just sorry he couldn't keep TQ alive long enough to witness the power of life and death that he had over all of TQ and Manny's families. TQ didn't whimper or beg – it wouldn't do any good. He kept his eyes on Ricco's face and his prayers toward heaven, trusting God. TQ would not give Ricco any pleasure from his evil actions.

Instead, to Ricco's frustration, TQ broke out in a song of praise to God in his native Navaho language in his best baritone voice. The pigeons that roosted on the little chapel in the village below suddenly took wing and flew low over the little group of men.

Ricco in an uncontrollable rage, shouted for TQ to stop singing. He pointed the automag at TQ and tried to shout over the songs of praise in the fine baritone which kept getting louder and louder. His fury was mounting, his evil was soaring, his threats were so horrible that the three men holding TQ were turning their heads away as if that action would keep them from hearing Ricco's rantings.

There no longer was a battlefield beyond them. All those previously enemies had risen together, turned, and stared at the scene unfolding beyond normal rifle range. All were powerless to save TQ. No one moved. What was happening was beyond the scope of the imagination of these seasoned fighting men.

Ricco brought his weapon in line, sighting down the barrel to a spot just above TQ's nose when his eyes were drawn away to the wink of light more than five hundred yards away. His eyes strained, his face went slack and he slowly whispered, "Nooo!"

Ken, a.k.a. Spooky, had struggled against a weak body, rock, brush, and not so fresh wounds to gain a position in the rocks for the best view of the waning battle, now nearly silent and still except for TQ's song and the shrill yelling of Ricco as they played out these tense moments of a fleeting life. He heard the maniacal laughter and shrill raging of Ricco as TQ raised his voice in praise of God with an unsurpassed beauty in his native tongue.

Spooky was positioned between two large rocks and resting the rifle on a smaller rock. As he looked through the scope, he thought briefly of the numbers of people executed by his uncanny skills with a rifle. Another breath, held it as the rifle fastened unwaveringly on the bridge of Ricco's nose. Ricco had become still, staring back at Spooky from over five hundred yards away. Spooky gently put even pressure on the trigger until the rifle jumped slightly in his hands. He looked through the scope again and saw TQ struggling to stand by himself as the three mercenaries were running away. Ricco was not in the sight picture of his rifle scope. His body had fallen behind some rocks as his spirit had gone to be confronted by God.

Suddenly, Ken realized God had used the gift he had with the rifle for the last time. He felt good, alive, for the first time in a long time. He struggled to his feet and decided against leaving the big weapon where children or anyone else could find it and misuse it. He turned down the path he had come up and said out loud, "Thank you, God. Girls, I'm coming home to stay." Subconsciously, he viewed himself taking the rifle apart and throwing the pieces over the side of Miguel's boat into the Pacific Ocean. Spooky and the rifle would be gone forever!

62
Family Forever

Twenty-two days later, Ken was turning the corner of his little adobe house for a brisk morning walk on the sandy beach when TQ's voice quietly asked, "Do you mind if I tag along?"

Spooky felt one second of fear. Then, Ken said, "Glad to have you. Guess we have a lot to talk about."

TQ, "Only if you want to. We have prayed. You are forgiven and part of God's family, our family. Anne insisted I invite your family to our annual Fourth of July party. Could you bring a pinata for the kids, and your appetites? We have everything else covered. If you like it there, there will be room for your family to settle. Become part of our family again."

TQ threw a big arm over Ken's shoulders as they walked peacefully along the sandy shore, quietly looking at the sun rising from the East and white, puffy clouds rolling across the sky. TQ looking toward heaven started teaching Ken, "In Lamentations it says, 'Through the Lord's mercies we are not consumed, because his compassions fail not. They are new every morning; great is your faithfulness, Oh God.' Those mercies are for everyone, for me and you."

Quietly Ken spoke. "My father would quote that verse every day.

Back then, it would irritate me. Now it gives me peace." He raised one hand toward the bright blue morning sky and saluted the Creator. A new soldier in God's army. Then he asked, "Who is this Indian woman with the long braids I've heard so much about?"

TQ pointed to the clouds as they swirled, moved, and came together as a figure only God could create. "You ever seen the picture of my mother that I have always carried with me?" TQ pulled the picture from his wallet and pointed with it to the clouds. God had moved the clouds to paint a perfect image of the lady in the picture TQ held. "Of all the people who saw her, ones she helped, smiled at, or talked to, no one ever touched her, never knew where she came from or where she went. My mom died when I was very young. I think God allowed her to come back and take care of me and those I love most. I think of her as a spirit from God. Others would call her a ghost. In God's word, it says, 'Be not forgetful to entertain strangers; for thereby some have entertained angels unawares.'"

They were smiling as they turned back up the beach and headed to the first of many family reunions as part of the family of God.

Biography

As a Chief Warrant Officer in the U.S. Army, K. Raymond Rush spent twenty years in places like Vietnam, Thailand, Somalia and numerous locations around the world. To relieve fear and frustration participants of war vent to colleagues whenever the adrenaline flows or they are drunk, high or longing for home. Mr. Rush has a good memory and an imagination to turn hearsay and experiences into a great adventure story.